LOST IN
ZOMBIELAND

The Rise of President Zero

LOST IN
ZOMBIELAND

The Rise of President Zero

A Political Satire

J.T. Hatter

Lionshare
lionsharepublishing.com

Ordering Information:
Quantity sales. Special discounts are available on quantity purchases by corporations, associations, and others. For details, contact the publisher at the address below.

Lionshare Publishing, LLC
P.O. Box 4100
Brentwood, TN 37024

Interior book design by David Moratto

Printed in the United States of America

First Printing

ISBN-13: 978-1470165222
ISBN-10: 1470165228
LCCN: 2012904262

This work is dedicated to people everywhere who seek Truth, Liberty, Justice and Freedom.

CONTENTS

INTRODUCTION

The great wonder of contemporary American politics is how Barack Hussein Obama got elected to the Office of President in the first place. It is a curiosity, to say the least. After three and a half years of getting to know the mysterious stranger in the White House, Americans are wondering why they voted for Obama. Voter remorse has never been higher and we are still troubled by serious questions that refuse to go away:

- Is Barack Obama a natural born citizen? Is he even eligible to be president?
- Why can't we see his college transcripts or get to the bottom of his multiple social security numbers? Why is he so secretive about his past?
- Is Obama trying to transform America into a socialist state?
- Why are his programs and policies so destructive?
- What is Obama really up to?

Nobody outside of Obama's inner circle knows the answer to these questions.

***

Obama's life experiences and beliefs are strange and unfamiliar to ordinary Americans. Any inquiry into his past becomes a journey into a land of unicorns and Alinsky, leftist indoctrination and black liberation theology, radicalism and the politics of race. Obama's mysterious origins and history might be amusing if their implications were not so serious.

But we Americans do not dwell exclusively on the serious. We have in our national DNA an eagerness to look on the humorous side of things, and to laugh out loud at ourselves—and especially at our politicians. Like no other nation on earth, we mercilessly lampoon, spoof, tease, expose, lambaste, roast and ridicule our political leaders. Most of them richly deserve what they get.

We've had great fun with Nixon, Carter, Reagan, Clinton and Bushes I and II. And now it's Obama's rightful turn. American society is infinitely improved when we carefully scrutinize our elected officials and measure them against our standards for justice and reason. And especially when we examine them through the bold lens of satire.

No president before Barack Hussein Obama has created such a satire-rich political environment for himself. In addition to his blundering policies, he has populated his administration with a rogue's gallery of radical characters and clowns. Under Obama, American government has become a circus—a surreal Kafkaesque wonderland of farce and fable. We are the bewildered guests at the Mad Hatter's tea party. Up is down and down is up. No one takes our government seriously any more.

It is true that Obama inherited a terrible mess from his predecessors. But Obama was voted in to fix these problems and restore the ship of state instead of running it headlong into the iceberg of reality. The administration's inexperience, bungling, cover-ups, corruption, incompetence, blind ideology, destructiveness and unintended comic relief are of truly historic dimension.

The Obama administration is a target-rich environment for critical commentary, but it is also a minefield for those who dare to tread within striking distance. Critics of the regime are automatically slandered as racist and savaged in the digital courtrooms of the mainstream media. Freedom of speech carries a steep price in today's politically correct America. But even these grave offenses can be made to boomerang under the magnifying lens of satire.

I would like to thank Obama's Marxist mentor, Saul Alinsky, for providing the political framework for this book, and especially for *Rules for Radicals* Tactics Rule No. 5:

> "Ridicule is man's most potent weapon. It is almost impossible to counterattack ridicule. Also, it infuriates the opposition, who then react to your advantage."

The most biting satire wields the sting of truth at its core. George Orwell, author of the famed dystopia, Nineteen Eighty-Four, with its culture of doublespeak and Big Brother, said, "During times of universal deceit, telling the truth becomes a revolutionary act."

This book is a revolutionary act. We live in a time when those who love the United States of America must fight to preserve her sacred truths and founding principles. The Tree of Liberty requires refreshment once again.

The Patriots of Lost in Zombieland have heard the call, and we charge into the breech, armed with cynicism and satire, to battle the dark forces of progressive politics. Our powder is dry, our flasks are full, and our humor is primed and ready.

— John Thompson Hatter

LOST IN
ZOMBIELAND
The Rise of President Zero

Life is hard. It's even harder when you're stupid.

—John Wayne

1

GROUND ZERO

"What do you mean the Iranians have a nuclear bomb?" President Omeba demanded.

The aides and military personnel in the Situation Room looked at him in surprise, then quickly turned back to their duties at a glare from Rahm. They'd informed the President two days ago that the Iranians had manufactured three, twenty-kiloton nuclear bombs, and were secretly moving the warheads to their targets: presumably in Israel, Europe and the United States.

"They made three of them," Leon Panera reminded the President. "We're trying to find them. That's the crisis."

The Secretary of Defense turned and looked around the Situation Room. It was crowded with high-ranking military officers, intelligence technicians and members of the President's Inner Circle.

"Where's General Dimpey? We need him in here to brief the President," Panera said.

An aide scuttled off to find the Chairman of the Joint Chiefs of Staff.

"What does the United Nations say about this?" President Omeba asked.

"They've confirmed it," Panera said. He didn't look happy about it. "The Iranians do have nuclear weapons. The economic sanctions didn't work. They never do."

"I thought the UN denied the Iranians were even working on a bomb," Omeba said. "They told us the Iranians were developing a peaceful nuclear program."

"Some people even believed that," Panera observed. "But it turned out that the IAEA Inspector General, Mohammed El Hussein, was working for the Muslims."

"No kidding? Who'd have expected that?"

"Well, sir," Panera confided, "The intelligence community has known about it for some time. We had to get past the racial profiling thing. But once we did that, we could see that Mohammed was helping the Islamic world acquire nuclear weapons: first the Iraqis under Saddam, and then the Iranians. He worked for the highest bidder. We knew the Iranians were building nuclear weapons, and we knew the UN was in cahoots with them. But the CIA couldn't get anybody in Congress or the White House to do anything about it. We just sat there and watched them start their nuclear program, build their centrifuges, refine the uranium and assemble their bombs. It's all George Boosh's fault, of course. He didn't do anything about it either."

"President Boosh's fault. Goes without saying," Omeba said. "On second thought, we better get out a press release, Leon. Tell the media to push the Boosh button on this Iranian bomb thing. They'll know what you mean."

"Yessir. Will do. Here's General Dimpey. He'll have an update on military intelligence."

General Dimpey arrived in the Situation Room with a bevy of intelligence officers and technicians in his wake. The four-star army General spotted Panera's beckoning finger, and joined the President and his Inner Circle. He waved his staff to their Situation Room workstations.

"Evening, General Dimpey," President Omeba said. "What's up with the Iranians?"

General Dimpey gave the President and Secretary Panera a deep frown, then nodded to Chief of Staff Rahm Adramelech and Senior Advisor Valerie Garrotte as they took their seats together at the conference table.

"Here it is in a nutshell, Mr. President," General Dimpey began. "The Iranians have built three nuclear bombs. Each has a yield of about twenty kilotons. We're finding out that the Iranians had a lot of technical help building the weapons, and they're getting logistical help moving them to the launch or target areas."

"Help?" Leon Panera asked. "Who's helping them?"

"Well, the Pakistani and North Korean governments have been supplying technicians, tools and materials to build the centrifuges and isotope processing systems. The Chinese are providing the isotope refining technology, and the Russians assisted in assembling the warheads. They're getting logistical help from the Egyptians and Syrians. Probably others. What we have here is a Communist/ Muslim axis."

"The Axis of Evil?" Omeba snickered. "Not that old Booshism again."

"It's *not* a laughing matter, Mr. President," the General replied. "Our intelligence sources think the Iranians are targeting Israel and the United States, and that they do intend to detonate the nuclear bombs as soon as they can get them to their targets."

Rahm and Valerie looked at one another. This was a very serious matter indeed. The National Security Council should be informed at once. A nuclear detonation in Israel would start another war in the Middle East. Hundreds of thousands of American lives were at risk. Possibly millions. But more importantly, if an atomic bomb actually detonated in the United States, then President Omeba's chances for reelection would go up in a nuclear smoke ring.

"I need a round of golf," President Omeba declared, wiping his forehead. The Iranian threat was serious business. If the Iranians did detonate a nuclear bomb in an American city, it might be enough to get the American people to look up from their high-definition, flat-screen television sets, and actually focus on *him*. This was serious business.

The elevator door opened and a tall, dark military officer strode into the Situation Room. The newcomer had a firm, measured step and an assured way about him. His face was deeply tanned. His sharp eyes swept the room and quickly locked onto General Dimpey.

"Excuse me, Mr. President," General Dimpey said. He went forward to greet the new arrival.

President Omeba wasn't pleased about being dismissed so abruptly. He didn't like the military. It was an article of progressive faith that the military must be loathed — unless you had control over it. Then you could tolerate it, use it as a tool for social engineering, or use it to put down social unrest.

Vice President Joe Bidet took his seat at the conference table.

"That's Colonel Plummer," the Vice President informed the Inner Circle. He nodded toward the officer who had just drawn General Dimpey away from them.

"He's quite a hero in military intelligence circles. He's heading up the military/CIA intelligence effort to locate and neutralize the nuclear weapons headed our way."

"I don't like him," Rahm said. He sized up the plethora of military decorations and campaign badges on the man's uniform with a look of utter disdain. Military men could not be trusted. Rahm didn't trust anyone he couldn't bribe or blackmail.

Valerie Garrotte, on the other hand, seemed quite taken with the new arrival. She drank in Colonel Plummer's strong military physique, his erect manner and his obvious intelligence. She took in the blue eyes and rich black hair that had just the right touch of gray at the temples. She felt a warm feeling beginning to spread just below her navel.

"Yummmm," she said, half to herself. "I could be all over that!"

Vice President Bidet nodded in agreement.

General Dimpey led the Colonel over to the Inner Circle and introduced him. Colonel Plummer shook hands firmly all around until he came to President Omeba. They eyed one another warily, like two roosters sizing each other up. They detested one another at once. They shook hands perfunctorily.

"Do you have a report for me, Colonel?" President Omeba inquired. "As Commander in Chief of the armed forces, I require your military assessment of the situation."

"I suggest we go into the Operations Center," Colonel Plummer replied. "There are a few items we have on satellite and video that you should see."

"I've called in the rest of the Inner Circle...and the NSC," Rahm said. "They're arriving now. We can all go to the OpCenter together."

The National Security Council included President Barak Hussein Omeba and Vice President Joe Bidet; Rahm Adramelech, Chief of

Staff; Valerie Garrotte, Senior Advisor to the President; Tom Dunlyin, National Security Advisor; Hillary Clitman, Secretary of State; Leon Panera, Secretary of Defense; Janet Napolitburo, Secretary of Homeland Defense; and a dozen other senior administration officials and functionaries.

"What's going on with the Strait of Hormuz?" Hillary Clitman demanded. As Secretary of State, she had a critical interest in protecting European oil supplies and the stability of client Muslim governments in the region. Half of the Middle Eastern oil supply passed daily through the Strait of Hormuz. The satellite image she referred to showed a thin line of American warships across the narrow passage. Opposing the thin line, and a mile distant, was a swarm of hundreds of smaller vessels. Graphic indicators suggested the presence of over twenty Iranian submarines mixed among them.

"We can start with that item, Madame Secretary," Colonel Plummer said, indicating the large screen overhead. He cleared his throat to gain everyone's attention.

"I've met most of you," Colonel Plummer said. "But to those I have not yet had the pleasure...I'm Colonel Joel Plummer. I'm with Special Operations Command and I'm attached to the CIA Working Group on the Persian Bomb crisis."

"Do we have to call it that?" interrupted Eric Holdup, the Justice Department Attorney General. "It sounds racist and prejudicial."

Colonel Plummer ignored him and continued with his presentation.

"The Secretary of State has pointed out one of the problems the Iranians are presenting us with," he said. "We think they're going to swarm the US Navy fleet defending the Strait of Hormuz. That would shut down the waterway and stop about half of the Gulf oil that normally goes to Europe and Asia. But that's not the real problem. We think the threat to the Hormuz Strait is a diversion to cover the movement of the three Persian Bombs." Colonel Plummer paused to give President Omeba a look. "Everyone will be focused on protecting the oil stream, or getting it started flowing again if the Iranians *do* try a military blockade or attack. The world won't be focused on what the Iranians are really up to — but *we* will be."

Plummer nodded to the technician to switch the view on the monitor. The next image was a map of the Middle East showing Iran, Iraq, Saudi Arabia, Syria, Jordan, Lebanon and Israel.

"The Iranians have already started what the Revolutionary Guard are calling 'The Path of the Mahdi'. If you don't already know, the Iranians have constructed three nuclear weapons, which they have already fielded. One is heading for Israel and the target is Tel Aviv. The Mossad is all over that one. There's a good chance they can intercept it before it gets to Tel Aviv. That bomb is currently in the Bekkah Valley in Lebanon. It's on a truck at a Hamas terrorist training center, or was a couple of hours ago."

The image zoomed in on a fertile agricultural valley in Lebanon, about twenty miles east of Beirut. Twenty large Quonset huts and innumerable tents sat nestled together in a rural setting. This was identified as the Hamas camp.

"Another bomb is heading for the United States. We think it's on a ship headed for the Mediterranean via the Suez Canal. We think the target is either New York or Washington, D.C. We have no idea where the third bomb is. The political analysts think it could be heading for Europe, but that's just conjecture. It really could be going anywhere."

Gasps and groans escaped the group. As senior government and military staff, they had seen many crises come and go, but this was the most terrifying they had yet encountered. Many of them realized that at least one of the three bombs would likely be detonated. And that could start World War III.

"Why don't we know where the other two bombs are? How can we be sure they're coming our way?" Vice President Bidet asked.

"Well, sir," Colonel Plummer answered. "Our intelligence community was forced to give up human intelligence — what we call humint — by the Clitman administration. As a result, we now have poor intelligence resources in much of the world, and especially in the Middle East. We're relying on the Israelis for most of our intel."

"I don't understand why we don't know where *our* bomb is," Hillary Clitman steamed. "If the Jews know where their bomb is, then we should know where *ours* is. We might even have two bombs coming our way. I think the Jews are behind this."

"The *Israelis*," Colonel Plummer corrected, "are our best source of intelligence and absolutely our best allies in this crisis. They've told us that if they can locate and capture the other bombs, then they will do so. But their first priority has to be the one addressed to Tel Aviv. We can't wait for their help. We have to find and capture the other two bombs ourselves if we can."

"How big are these bombs?" Leon Panera asked.

"Twenty kilotons each," Plummer answered. "They should weigh about a ton each, so we're not talking about suitcase nukes. These are big bombs."

"Twenty kilotons doesn't sound like much," Panera commented. "I thought nukes were measured in megatons."

"A twenty kiloton nuke has a blast radius of half a mile," Plummer replied. "That's ground zero. Everything in that blast radius is vaporized. Mortality is one hundred percent. Out from ground zero there is a severe damage radius of about a mile. Mortality is eighty percent. Out from that, the damage radius extends to about five miles. Total mortality in the affected area is about seventy five percent. We expect about two and a half million deaths and at least that many casualties if the device is detonated in New York City. After the initial blast, the radioactive fallout and secondary effects will claim at least a million more lives. The entire city will burn uncontrollably. New York City will be no more."

The Situation Room was deathly silent. The senior staffers and technicians pondered what it would mean to have the nation's most populous city suddenly destroyed by the jihadi forces of Islam. The Muslims had successfully attacked New York in the past. The Islamic attack of 9/11 claimed over three thousand American lives, and was still vividly remembered.

New York City was a natural target for America's enemies. It was a communications and investment center, a hub of world commerce. The United Nations was in New York. Major banks and corporations had their headquarters there. What would happen to the national economy if it were destroyed? What would happen to the people living in the region? They sat in shock and disbelief as they pondered the implications of a successful enemy nuclear strike. It was too horrible to imagine.

"Okay," Janet Napolitburo said. "As Secretary of Homeland Defense, I've got to do something about New York. We've got to get emergency response units up to speed and prepare medical and security personnel just in case this does happen."

"New York City is a peninsula, Ms. Napolitburo," Colonel Plummer said. "You've got to cross the Hudson or East Rivers to get to most of it. Most of the city will be on fire. The radioactivity will be intense. Nobody will be able to approach the city for weeks. I'm glad that rescue and relief isn't my job. My job is to stop the bombs from arriving at our shores. That's what we're working on right now. The Persian Bomb Task Force planners will give you a more detailed briefing in a few moments. My Special Forces teams are deploying to the Middle East to find and neutralize the bombs. I ask that you give us your absolute best efforts when we call on you for help. We will need each of you for diplomatic, political and logistical support, I fear, before this is over. Remember this request. It is important. I may call on you personally for your support when the going gets tough. Thank you for your valuable time. Now if you'll excuse me..."

Colonel Plummer nodded to the President's team and made to leave the Situation Room. But at a signal from President Omeba, Rahm cadged the military officer over to the end of the conference table. The Inner Circle had risen from the table and stood together in a huddle.

"Yes, Mr. Adramelech?" Colonel Plummer said.

"One moment. The President wants to have a word with you. And I want to give you my personal assurance that you'll have our fullest cooperation and support on this mission," Rahm said. The other members of the Inner Circle gave murmurs of assurance and nods in the affirmative. President Barak Hussein Omeba stepped forward. Everyone expected words of encouragement and support for the fine military officer who had just briefed them. President Omeba took the full measure of the uniform and the man before he spoke.

"Go get me a mocha," President Omeba ordered.

Colonel Plummer looked at him.

"I'm the Commander in Chief," Omeba said, looking coldly at the military man. "You obey my orders. Now go get me a mocha. And sprinkle some nutmeg and cinnamon on it. Not too much, or I'll send you back to the kitchen again. Make it snappy."

General Dimpey had a horrified expression on his face. He knew the Special Forces Colonel who was standing a mere killing blow away from the President. He knew that Colonel Plummer did not suffer fools lightly, and that he had no fear of fools who out-ranked him.

"You know," Colonel Plummer said to the President, looking him full in the face, "most people in the armed forces think that you live in a make-believe world; that you don't live in the same reality as the rest of us. I see now that this is true. But I have to live in the real world. And in that world our Islamic enemies have constructed nuclear bombs they intend to explode in major cities — perhaps Washington, D.C. itself. So you get your own mocha, Mr. President. I've got nuclear warheads to find."

He stepped back, gave the President a salute, turned and walked to the elevators.

"Insubordinate military trash!" Rahm spat. "Don't worry, Mr. President. I'll send him to the Aleutians for his insolence. He needs to learn some respect."

"You do that, Rahm," the President said. "We can't have military officers showing disrespect to our office. We've had to sack a couple dozen of them already for this sort of thing. You'd think by now that they'd have gotten the message."

"It's the Neanderthal military mentality," Hillary observed. "They're all like that. You can't imagine the problems we had with them when Bill and I held the White House. Why...they never even let us have a top security clearance. The nerve of those morons. Send the Secret Service after him. Colonel Plummer needs to be taught who's in command. Off with his head!"

General Dimpey spoke up. "Don't stop him, Mr. President. I apologize for his behavior and I'll have him apologize to you personally. But right now we desperately need him. Colonel Plummer is our best man. He may be the only one who can avert tragedy and possibly war — even World War III. Let him go. *Please*, Mr. President."

Omeba gave the four-star general a disdainful sneer; then nodded in acquiescence to his pleading.

"Very well, General Dimpey," President Omeba said. "I'll let him go this time. He can give me a full apology and face a court-martial after this is over. That works for me."

"Thank you, Mr. President," the general said. "I meant it when I said how much we need Colonel Plummer. If anyone can find the bastards and their bombs he can. He's hot on their trail right now."

"That's all fine, General Dimpey," the President said coldly. "But if he fails, I'll court-martial both of you."

"Yessir."

"And General...I still want a mocha. Lightly sprinkled with nutmeg and cinnamon. Step right down to the kitchen and pick that up for me, will you?"

2

THE INNER CIRCLE

The Inner Circle had a floating membership, but the core members were Valerie Garrotte, Rahm Adramelech, Leon Panera, Janet Napolitburo, Eric Holdup and Vice President Joe Bidet. The President's advisors huddled around the conference table in the Situation Room to make political decisions about the current military crisis.

"Mr. President," Rahm said. "This is a national emergency of the highest order. The Persian Bomb crisis will take all of our military and government resources. We won't have time for anything else until this is over. This is a disaster."

President Omeba looked irritated.

"I agree," he said. "My reelection campaign should be receiving our full attention and all our national resources. We haven't got time for this Persian Bomb thing. We need to round up these nuclear bombs and make the situation go away. I'll call the President of Iran and see if I can get the Iranians to take them back."

"Yessir," Rahm replied. "But we can't let this crisis go to waste. This is just too good an opportunity to pass up."

"We need something quick, Rahm," Valerie said. "I've got the new poll numbers."

"Let's have it," Omeba ordered.

"A generic Republican will win by twenty two percent. *Any* Republican, Mr. President," Valerie Garrotte said. "We have a real crisis on our hands."

President Omeba was horrified.

"I can't believe it's that bad," he uttered, disbelief clear in his voice.

"I can," Rahm said. "Lush Rimshot is on the radio all day long running our administration down and calling us names. He's shedding a lot of light on what we're actually doing. To make matters worse, Fox News is reporting actual news events instead of getting in line like the rest of the media. It's disgraceful. Then there's Ben Gleck, Hans Sanity and all the rest of those conservative talk show radio blowhards. People listen to them. They're having an impact. Especially Lush Rimshot."

"It's the Tea Partiers too," Valerie said. "Those private sector workers are going to cost us the election if we don't do something about them. Our RINOs can't control them."

"Those bitter racists again? Still clinging to their guns and bibles I bet. Why can't they just let the government help them?" Omeba asked, genuinely perplexed. "We can change their minds if they'll just start taking government checks. Why can't they cooperate with us a little?"

"I don't know, Barry," Rahm replied. "I'm from Chicago. I just don't understand people who won't take money for their votes."

President Omeba shook his head negatively. This was a problem.

"We've got to do something about them and soon. Something effective. I have to be reelected. I have to be. And it's your job to make that happen."

He stabbed a finger at both of them. Rahm and Valerie nodded. The fundraising machine was doing a bang up job gathering campaign money. The TARP and Stimulus trillions were paying off big time. But their voter base had evaporated in the last three years, due largely to President Omeba's policies and actions. And no matter how much money they spent, about half of the American people just couldn't be bought. The situation was getting desperate.

Omeba's approval ratings were stuck below forty-five percent — the death zone for a politician seeking reelection. The economy was crashing, largely because of Omeba's fiscal and energy policies. And there was no light at the end of the dark economic tunnel he had driven the nation further into. Valerie's new poll numbers spelled doom for their entire political agenda. If they didn't do something soon, the American people could regain control of their government.

An aide came into the room and whispered in Vice President Bidet's ear. Joe Bidet closed his eyes and groaned.

"They're outside again," Bidet complained. "We're surrounded."

Rahm and Valerie looked at one another.

"Who? The Iranians?" demanded the President.

"No," Bidet sputtered. "It's the *people*! They're marching again! The Secret Service says it looks serious this time. There's a big crowd out there today. Let's go look."

They left the Situation Room. Joe Bidet led the way to the elevators and across the concourse to the White House. They gathered on the third floor and looked across the north lawn to Pennsylvania Avenue. Sure enough, the streets and sidewalks were filled with angry protesters.

"What are all those people doing out there?" President Omeba complained. They looked out the White House windows at the huge throngs of people swarming below. It was an angry crowd. Omeba could not believe they were actually out there like this, marching up and down Pennsylvania Avenue in front of the White House, waving picket signs and singing patriotic songs. The news media might actually report this.

"Yep," Rahm said. "It's the Tea Party protesters again. Taxed Enough Already. The Tea Baggers look plenty pissed out there today. Look at them."

Valerie Garrotte, Joe Bidet, Rahm Adramelech, Tom Dunlyin and President Omeba watched the crowd wave their picket signs and march up and down the streets.

"I really don't know why these people are getting so riled up over taxes anyway, President Omeba said. "It's not like they've got anything better to do with their money. What could be better than my health plan? My jobs bill?"

The President looked across the north lawn to Pennsylvania Avenue. One marcher in particular irritated him. The man carried a sign that said 'The Only Way to Cut Spending is to Cut Democrats!'

Omeba waggled a finger at a Secret Service agent, who came quickly over to him. Omeba pointed out the protester to him.

"See that man with the sign?" he asked.

"Yessir. I see him."

"If I told you to go shoot him, would you do it?"

"Ah...I'd have to check with my supervisor, sir," the agent demurred.

Omeba shook his head. He knew what the answer would be. He'd been down this road before.

"Never mind. I want you to forget we had this conversation. Understand?"

"Yessir."

But the protester really bothered him. *All* of these protesters bothered him. They were in his face. They kept coming back to Washington every time he did something important.

The first bunch of protesters had flooded downtown Washington six months after Omeba's inauguration. It was a new group called the Tea Party. Nearly a quarter of a million miscreants gathered in front of the White House to protest the taxation and spending policies of the Democratic Party. Where had they been the last fifty years? The protesters were furious over the Stimulus Plan that he had rammed through Congress. About a quarter of the picket signs had some reference to stimulus spending.

Omeba was certain that the legislative fiat would enable him to purchase reelection. He doled out over five trillion dollars to Democratic Party supporters using money borrowed from China. He and the Democrats had put America another five trillion dollars in debt for the worthy cause of ensuring that the Democratic Party stayed in power. Lush Rimshot and the other radio patriots dubbed the program, 'porkulous', which was not an entirely inaccurate description.

Then came the dreaded Taxpayer March on Washington three months later. Washington again filled up with hundreds of thousands of protesters. They poured in like lemmings. Those protesters were trying to derail his signature issue, the Patient Protection and Affordable Care Act — OmebaCare. He was insanely proud of that act.

OmebaCare ensured that America would enter the twenty-first century in step with her socialist European cousins. OmebaCare was the straw that would break America's capitalist backbone, and render the Constitution meaningless. The United States would be forced to abandon both the archaic capitalist economic system, and the odious Constitution that had hindered progressive government in the nation since its inception.

It was a tough fight to get OmebaCare passed through both houses of Congress, but he managed it with Democrat majorities in both houses, generous bribes, underhanded deals and unconstitutional legislative maneuvers. Not a single Republican in the House or Senate voted for OmebaCare, and the reactionaries were already working to end it. Twenty-six states sued the federal government to have the law repealed. More than any government action since the War Between the States, this one effectively divided the nation and pitted Americans against one another. It was his crowning achievement.

The dreaded Tea Partiers showed up to protest and derail OmebaCare — more than eight hundred thousand of them. Omeba ignored them. Or tried to. The problem was that they wouldn't admit defeat and go away. The Tea Partiers were more than a nuisance; they were becoming positively dangerous. Even the relentless media slander had neither discredited nor stopped them. The Tea Party protests just kept getting bigger and louder. Worse, they had grown political teeth and showed that they could bite hard.

In the mid-term elections, the Democrats lost the House of Representatives under a tsunami of protest voters who'd had enough. But Omeba held onto the Senate, and it became his power base. He hoped it would be enough to get more of his agenda passed. But by the look of the size and temperament of the crowd outside, he was no longer sure he could get *any* more legislation through Congress. Things might be past the point of no return. He had a bad feeling about those protesters.

But they weren't about to stop Omeba's radical agenda. They said he had a tin ear. They didn't understand. It wasn't even a question of having a tin ear. Omeba was a man on a mission. He had no intention of listening to anyone.

"The unwashed masses out there," Omeba said, indicating the throng below. "They don't understand me. They have no idea who I am...what I represent. Why don't they realize that I am the hope and change they need? Why can't these ignorant, stubborn people see who I am?"

His advisors remained silent. His narcissistic flights and dark moods were becoming more frequent and more intense. That worried them. They looked nervously at one another. The mass demonstrations always upset him. President Omeba turned to Tom Dunlyin and looked at him with wide eyes.

"Tom, do you realize what would happen to this country if something should happen to *me?*"

"Economic recovery, sir?"

"No, you jackass. Joe Bidet becomes President."

"I see what you mean. That would be a disaster."

"And if Joe and I get killed together — say Air Force One goes down on the way to Pebble Beach — then it's Hillary in the White House. The Secretary of State is third in line."

"Oh my," Tom said. "What kind of a fool put her in that position? Hillary? In the White House? That would bring Bill Clitman back."

"Exactly!" Omeba cried. "He would suck the political oxygen out of Washington forever. Not to mention what would happen to all the female interns. And suppose something happened to Hillary. Who's next in the line of succession?"

"Um. That would be the Secretary of the Treasury, sir. Tim Geitmare."

President Omeba shook his head.

"That guy can't even do his own tax returns. The nation is screwed. Do you see what I mean?" Omeba asked.

"Yessir," Tom agreed, straightening up. "You are far too important to lose. Your agenda is too important. No one else can carry the torch for the unwashed masses. They need someone to dazzle them with media sound bites, collect their votes and lead them to the feed trough. We need four more years so that you can consolidate your power, sir. For the long haul. There's an awful lot that has to be done. We're really just getting started being transformational."

"You're right as usual, Tom," the President said. "I'm too important to be denied a second term — regardless of the will of the people. We know better than they what they need. We'll have to do whatever it takes to win reelection."

"That's absolutely correct, sir. Whatever it takes."

"*We* are the ones that we have been waiting for," Omeba said quietly, half to himself.

He walked to the White House window and looked out over the north lawn again. The crowds were out there milling about, shouting and waving their pathetic signs. He despised them all, the ingrates — the uneducated, racist, unwashed horde. They opposed him. The polls showed that more than half of the American people utterly rejected his policies and programs. How dare those little people out there oppose him?

He was *The One*. Barak Hussein Omeba was The One that they had been waiting for.

3

THE ONE

Omeba looked lovingly into the mirror. He smiled at the thousand-watt grin beaming back at him. Barak loved to look at his face. And he knew that millions of other people loved to look at him too. Barak could not blame them. He was beautiful, after all. His skin was pecan tan — light for a first generation African American. His mother was a white American and his father was a Kenyan. His face was open and sincere-looking. His ears stood wide from his head, which bothered him. To his dismay, his ears had become the focal point of every political cartoonist in the world. They gave him a startling resemblance to Alfred E. Neuman.

He admired his mouth. It was his single greatest asset. Omeba had a mouth of power. The words that issued from it were like magic to fully half of those who heard him speak. He loved to speak and he loved to hear himself speak. Everyone else did too. Nearly everyone. His speech had a mesmerizing power, at least for liberals. They could not resist his words. They drank his words like fine wine. His words inebriated them.

His pecan tan skin was his second greatest asset. With his skin color he could evoke liberal guilt and sympathy — a powerful force in a society dominated by progressive media, education and government. His Vice President, Joe Bidet, had once remarked that Omeba was "...the first mainstream African-American who is articulate and bright and clean and a nice-looking guy. I mean; that's storybook, man." Lush Rimshot had dubbed him *The Magic Negro* in a song parody. And he was magic. Everything about him seemed to be magical.

Brilliant oratory was his forte. His ability to speak to the hearts of guilty liberals was the source of all his success and power. He had the gift and knew it. His fellow students at Harvard nicknamed him *Deepthroat* because of his silver-tongued talent. Omeba once brought a crowd to its feet in a raucous, enthusiastic cheer *after* he had finished speaking. He turned away to grab a tissue, and indelicately turned back to the crowd and blew his nose. The people roared their approval, giving him a standing ovation for his effort.

Omeba had a peculiar effect on liberals and they responded to him in strange ways. Some felt a thrill going up their legs when he spoke. Others felt mesmerized, as if they'd been hypnotized or drugged. His more giddy followers felt his presence as a mystical experience of a semi-religious nature, as if they were in the presence of a powerful demi-god. They believed that he could control the forces of nature. They were enthralled by the sound of his voice. They behaved like zombies: hanging on his every word, worshipping him openly, following him mindlessly, obeying his every suggestion and command, and giving no thought to the reality of the world they lived in.

But Barak was not universally loved. Those at the political center and on the right could see right through him. Omeba was easier to see through than Senator John Swiftboat (who served in

Vietnam) or Vice President Al Bore. To the moderate or conservative, Omeba was obviously a con artist, an impostor. He was the master illusionist on the public stage, and they could easily see through this tricks and misdirection. Liberals, however, swooned at his least gesture, and implicitly believed his every word.

Omeba was transparently a Marxist radical. He was a socialist. He refused to wear the American flag on his lapel or salute it when the national anthem was played, even after he was elected to public office. He was not proud to be an American and admitted as much openly until his presidential campaign. His colleagues unanimously affirmed that Barak Hussein Omeba was as pure a Marxist as there ever was. All of his ideas for hope and change involved transforming America from a capitalist representative republic to a Marxist socialist state. He made no secret of his plans.

Accordingly, he was excoriated by conservative radio talk show hosts, especially Lush Rimshot, Ben Gleck, Han Sanity and Phillipe Valentino. The argument against Omeba's policies and goals had nothing to do with his race. His black detractors blasted him as well, but for different reasons. The race-baiting Princeton University professor, Cornel Worst, called Barak an "inauthentic black man", because the Harvard- and Colombia-educated Omeba had grown up with middle class white privilege. He had not walked a mile in the moccasins of a "real" black man. This was true. The most famous race pimp in the nation, Jesse Jackass, said publicly that he wanted to cut Omeba's nuts off because of the way he talked *down* to black people.

Omeba was not black enough for some black liberals, and much too white for others. But he was the perfect color for the mainstream media. Once the mainstream media discovered Barak Hussein Omeba, they immediately and unanimously decided that he would be the next President of the United States. They had the means to interfere with the election process sufficiently to put him in office. They had done so with Bill Clitman, had near misses with Al Bore and John Swiftboat, and they were determined to do it again with Barak Hussein Omeba.

The media swooned over the new black liberal politician, an Alinsky community organizer from Chicago. He was Franklin Delano Roosevelt, John F. Kennedy and Martin Luther King all rolled into one. The news media were galvanized by the very idea of this attractive black socialist. He would be the first black American president. They would make him so. The media would make themselves a new President the same way they had made him a Senator.

The media collaborated and worked hard to support the newest Democrat star. They invested hundreds of millions to support his campaign. Omeba's candidacy ushered in an unprecedented tsunami of advocacy journalism. Television, radio, internet, magazine and newspaper journalists formed secret associations to pass along ideas for media campaigns to support their star. They worked closely with the Democratic National Party and Omeba campaign officials to coordinate their messaging to the public.

Like all liberals, the talking heads and other media workers were genuinely enthralled with Omeba. They followed him everywhere, capturing every useful utterance and favorable image. In terms of media coverage, Omeba was overexposed. Such a thing had never happened in American politics. Neither he, nor they, could get enough of each other.

By contrast, the Republican candidate for office, Juan McStain, was portrayed as yet another stingy, old white guy with Puritan values. He was a conservative member of the Washington establishment: the enemy. To liberal and conservative minds alike, this representation of Juan McStain was not altogether inaccurate.

The media depictions of the Democratic Party candidate, however, were fabricated out of fairy wings and pixie dust. They photoshopped together a personality construct for Omeba, basically making a Frankenstein media monster out of liberal ideals, icons and heroes. It bore no resemblance to the real Omeba. His true personality was not kind, personable and empathetic. In reality, he was malignant, egomaniacal and callous. The media projected a better image for him: one that would get him elected.

Barak Hussein Omeba was the least qualified candidate to ever run for the Presidency. He was, in fact, ineligible for the office. That he was neither qualified nor eligible for the most important elected office in the United States of America did not bother the media, nor stop them from campaigning for him. It did not stop the Democratic Party machine from wrenching the candidacy from an astonished Hillary Clitman, and awarding it to their Frankenliberal media creation.

The mainstream media wanted Omeba in the White House in the worst way. Barak was not merely the alternative to Hillary, who actually had a sliver of experience related to the office they both sought. He was the alternative to the conservative white Republican — the enemy. Omeba was the anti-Boosh. Omeba would strike a blow against the greedy, white, oppressor capitalists. He was the light worker who would bring hope and change to the American people, whether they wanted it or not.

The media studiously ignored his lack of experience and radical political associations, although they were well known. Barak was the most liberal senator in the U.S. Senate, even more liberal than Hillary herself. But this was not mentioned in the mainstream news coverage.

Omeba's only tangible accomplishments up to that point in his life were two books he had written about himself. He had no real accomplishments to write about, so he wrote about his personal "journey." It was enough for the news media, who didn't pry into his medical history, academic records, citizenship status, drug use, foreign travel, employment history, law career, multiple social security numbers, forged Selective Service card, love life or anything normally the object of intense interest to the media. How many people had seven social security numbers? How many presidential candidates attended college as a foreign student? The media decided it was best not to mention these things.

The Democrats faced a weakened Republican opposition. Nancy Perjuri and Red Harry, as leaders of the House and Senate, had spent the previous eight years tearing down the Republican presidency, and painting the worst possible picture of Republicans, labeling them the "culture of corruption". They got away with this despite the fact that the previous eight years were remarkably scandal free.

But after eight years of relentless slander and false witness by Red Harry, San Fran Nan and the mainstream media, the American people were ready to throw the Republican rascals out of office.

The timing worked brilliantly for the Democratic Party and the media. The American people were sick and tired of RINO foreign wars, taxation and spending, overregulation, crony capitalism, a new round of unfunded mandates, and generally running the government into the ground and acting like Democrats.

The American People sincerely hoped for change — *any* kind of change. After eight years of compassionate conservatism, the American people desperately needed change in their government. Washington was broken and everyone knew it.

It was the chance of a generation for the Democrats. Never before had the alignment of political forces, media influence, and cold hard cash come together to elect such an inexperienced, unqualified and untried candidate to the most powerful executive position in the world.

The American people elected Barak Hussein Omeba to the Presidency of the United States of America with fifty-three percent of the popular vote. Barak Hussein Omeba, with his beautiful, smiling, pecan tan face; his silver tongue; and his utter lack of meaningful experience, became the most powerful man on the planet.

He was a man on a mission, uniquely placed in time and office to do what countless others in the socialist sphere had so desperately wanted to do for so long: put the United States of America irrevocably on the path to becoming a socialist state.

Barak Hussein Omeba looked into the mirror again. There was a growing trace of doubt in that beautiful face. It had grown steadily since the fabled day he swore on the Holy Bible to uphold the Constitution and fulfill the requirements of the office. The United States had proved to be amazingly resistant to change. Doubt grew as to whether or not he could complete his mission in time. The cause of social justice and One World Government depended on him. The burden was heavy.

He looked deeper into those handsome, wonderful eyes. They twinkled back, assuring him. He had been given great power, and that power was within him. Of course he could do it. He was The One. The face shining back at him was beautiful. It was filled with hope and promise. People believed his face. They believed anything he told them. He was the most powerful man in the world. He possessed cunning and guile in abundance. He would tell the necessary lies. He would sign the decrees and laws necessary to the task. Nothing could withstand this face...his charming smile, the disarming personality. He was irresistible.

"BARAK HUSSEIN OMEBA!" a voice screeched behind him.

He jumped in stark, white terror; startled out of his wits.

"You standin' in front of that mirror admiring yo'self *again*?" his wife yelled, shaking her head derisively at him, her hands on her hips. "You got to be the most vain man I ever knew!"

He spun around. She hulked over him, her eyes wide and glaring, her face an angry scowl. Her powerful arms stood like tree limbs on the broad trunk of her hips. She caught him flat-footed in front of the mirror again. *Looking at the future*, he called it.

"I never seen a man so in love with hisself," she declared. "I bet when you was a little boy in Indonesia, you looked at yo'self in the mud puddles."

"Moochelle honey..."

"Don't you Moochelle honey *me*," she warned, shaking a clawed finger at him. She crossed her arms and bore down on him. "You got some 'splaining to do."

"Yes dear," he said. His shoulders slumped in resignation. "What do I need to explain this time?"

"I had lunch with the women of the Congressional Progressive Caucus."

"Oh yeah?" he asked, interested. The members of the CPC were feisty radicals. He liked them a lot, except when they were running their mouths on TV about him not doing what they wanted him to be doing.

"Yeah. They asked me what side you on."

"Oh. I'm getting that a lot lately. Mostly from the Republicans."

"You'd think they'd a' figgered that out by now."

"I know. They just can't believe it."

"Well, neither can the women of the CPC," Moochelle complained. "They want to know 'bout the OmebaCare funding. They say that snake John Boner has jerked out the fundin' for Planned Parenthood."

President Omeba backed up. He knew what was coming next. Trouble. He didn't know if he feared facing Moochelle or his own congressional party more on this toxic issue. Boner had snagged abortion funding away from Planned Parenthood, one of his pet programs. There would be hell to pay if his constituents couldn't get the government to pay for their abortions. Abortions were expensive.

"This is a matter of women's health, Barry," Moochelle said, bearing down on him. "You better get that fundin' back or I'll wear you out, so help me. I'll tan yo' hide."

"Don't get upset, dear," he said. He looked around to see if there was any way out of the dressing room in case she got physical. It was no use. She was stronger and faster than him.

"You *know* that abortion has always been my top priority," he said. He was on dangerous ground and knew it. Trying to reason with Moochelle was a tricky proposition. "We've got two daughters, Moose. If they make a mistake, I don't want them punished with a baby."

"Me neither," Moochelle agreed. But she was not satisfied. He had not answered her question. Both of them were lawyers. He wasn't going to get off that easy.

"John Boner pulled a fast one in the House yesterday," the President said. "But he won't get away with it. I'm holding up approval for the XL pipeline. I've suspended drilling in the Gulf of Mexico too. He can't get any oil from Alaska or the Interior Department either, unless I release the environmental permits. I've got him by the short hairs, Moochelle. If that doesn't work, I can cut military pensions. Don't worry. I've got this under control. We'll get our abortion funding back."

She scowled at him.

"I know how important this is, honey," the President said. He stifled a tendency to flinch when they were this close together. "Abortions and welfare are our bread and butter."

"I'll be watchin' you."

"I know, honey."

"I'll be watchin' you from Trinidad next week," she said.

"Trinidad? You going on another trip?" he asked hopefully.

"You bet. Can't wait to get outta Washington."

"Don't you like being First Lady?" he asked.

"Don't ask! It's hell. I can't stand it!"

"But, Moochelle," he protested. "I need to get reelected. That's four more years. I wish you liked being First Lady at least a little bit."

"Four more years of shoppin' and travelin' with my friends, you mean," she retorted. "This First Lady business is bullshit! Nobody takes me seriously. If I gotta be stuck doin' this, I'm gonna get me some payback."

"You've been doing that, honey."

"And I'm keepin' the dresses."

"Sure, Moose. You going to be gone long? We have a state dinner with the British Prime Minister and his wife next week."

"England?" she exclaimed. "I'm not cuttin' my trip short for those people."

"I understand. I'm not looking forward to it either. We've got the Australian Ambassador in town next week too."

"Still too British."

"Well, Sarkozy and his wife are going to be visiting at the end of the week."

"That bitch? Forget it," Moochelle spat. "You tell her sumpthin' and it's around the world before you can take your makeup off."

"Okay, Moochelle. Whatever you want. We'll make do. I'll tell everyone you're on an ambassadorial mission for the White House."

"Whatever."

"Moochelle," Omeba said delicately, careful not to ruffle feathers. "I wish you liked being First Lady more."

She glared at him, looking very much like the *Grinch Who Stole Christmas.*

"I *hate* it, I tole you," she snapped. "It's not like I thought it would be. I like the power...and all the gifts. We made millions at this...but I can't stand pretendin' to be nice all the time. I hate people followin' me around with a schedule others made up for me. I can't stand the reporters."

"They're on our side, honey," Barak reminded. "We need them."

"Sure, but I can't do nothin' I want like I used to. I gotta leave the country to have any privacy. It's no fun, Barry."

"It's only a little while longer, Moochelle. Then we'll be done."

"The rest of this term and four more years," Moochelle corrected. "Sometimes I wonder if it's worth it."

"Now, now," he said.

Omeba looked up at her. He tried to put his arms around her muscular arms and torso, but couldn't manage to reach all the way around.

"We've talked about this," he said to her. "We're on a mission, remember?"

He reached up to tilt her head down. He needed to look into her eyes instead of up her nose.

"Our Presidency is transformational." He looked deep into her eyes. He turned on the magic voice. "We worked all this out in

Chicago in our living room. With Valerie, Bill and Bernadine. Remember, honey? How we were going to transform the United States? We've just begun the journey, Moochelle. OmebaCare is the stake in the belly of the beast. But the beast can still recover.

"We've monetized the debt so the dollar is shot as a real currency, at least for now. Our stimulus spending has put the nation so far into debt that I don't see how it can ever recover — but it could if future generations pay down the debt and spend within their means. Moochelle, we've blasted a gigantic hole in the capitalist economic system, but that hole could be mended in time. We have to get the Cloward-Piven strategy solidly locked into place so they can't *ever* get out from under the debt load. That's a major battle I think we'll win, but there's so much more we have to do.

"We still have to deal with the military and the Constitution. We still have to get liberal educational programs established for the next generation of progressives. I need another term to get that all done. And I need you with me. If we're going to fundamentally change America, I need more time. I need four more years."

Moochelle looked at her husband with hooded eyes for a long time. She was immune to his charms. She knew him. But what he had said was true and important to the revolution. His motives were actually pure. She knew that. Omeba was not a thinker, despite the media portrayal of him as an intellectual genius. She knew that he was incapable of critical thinking of any kind. She also knew he lacked any sentiment whatsoever, except for himself.

Omeba was wholly motivated by the hard leftist propaganda he had absorbed from his mother, Occidental College, Colombia University, Harvard and the University of Chicago Law School — all bastions of progressive liberal programming. He received his religious instruction as a child in the Indonesian Basuki school as a Muslim; and as an adult from Reverend White, the infamous Chicago Black Liberation Theology firebrand. Revolution was his religion.

Barry was a community organizer at heart, and he was still trying to right the wrongs of the oppressors. She knew quite well where he was coming from. Barry was thoroughly indoctrinated into the liberal groupmind. She had received the same indoctrination herself. They were fellow travelers. This might be about Barry's ego to a large degree, but it had nothing to do with greed. Barry was a true believer.

"Okay Barry," she relented. "We want the same things. We want to make them pay. I'll give you the time you need. But you just remember one thing."

"What's that?"

"I'm on top now," she said coldly. "And I'm gonna to ride it for all it's worth." She turned to leave. "I'm gonna pack," she said. "I'll catch up to you *after* the revolution."

4

THE THIRTEENTH IMAM

Mahmoud Ahmanutjob believed that the Thirteenth Imam disappeared as a child during the eighth century, and had been dwelling at the bottom of a deep, hidden well ever since. He believed that one day the Thirteenth Imam would rise from the well and materialize as the all-powerful Mahdi — the one who would lead the Muslim faithful in a holy jihad against the rest of the world. The Mahdi would bring Armageddon to humanity, slaying billions of infidels, and subduing the survivors in perpetual dhimmitude under the bondage of the new global Caliphate. But the door of the well had to be opened before the Hidden Imam could emerge. The flaming path to jihad had to be prepared before he would come out of the well.

Mahmoud Ahmanutjob, President of The Revolutionary Republic of Iran, believed that he held the key to that door. The key was made of enriched uranium. The Holy Path of Flames led through the United States of America. Three burning Torches of Jihad had been sent forth: one destined for the monkeys and snakes in Tel Aviv, one for the United States, and a third whose destination was hidden.

Mahmoud was satisfied that destiny was being fulfilled. It would soon be over for the Great Satan. The entire world would enter the House of War and begin the long terrible struggle. But when the Thirteenth Imam emerged from the well and took his rightful place the head of the mujahideen armies, the world would be bathed in blood and fire, and the infidel world would fall. In time, the Caliphate would be established and all dhimmi nations, including the United States, would service their Muslim overlords. The entire world would bow before Allah. Mahmoud was confident of this. He was also confident of his reward in heaven.

He was savoring these delicious thoughts when his aide rushed into his office with a worried look on his face.

"You will not believe who is calling you. It is an urgent call. You must take it."

"Tell me who it is first," Ahmanutjob said, fearing a problem with the mullahs.

"It is the President of the United States."

"Again? What does that apostate dog want this time?" Ahmanutjob reached for his phone. "Barak? Is this you? Mahmoud here. How is my old friend?"

"Hi there, Mahmoud," Omeba's voice came in loud and clear over the President of Iran's private line. "Have you got a minute to chat?"

"Always for you, my friend." Ahmanutjob made a face at his aide. His aide crossed his eyes and stuck out his tongue. They did this with one another whenever a western leader called begging for something. "What can I do for you today?"

There was a pause on the line. Mahmoud pressed his ear into the receiver to see if he could hear if anything was being whispered to Omeba back in Washington, D.C. There was nothing. Omeba was alone. Then President Omeba spoke.

"Mahmoud, I've received some distressing news."

"Yes?"

"We've received intelligence reports that your government has manufactured some nuclear bombs and that they've left your borders," Omeba said. "Is this anything I need to be concerned about?"

Ahmanutjob froze. He was in a state of absolute shock. He had no idea the Americans knew about the bombs. It had to be the Israelis who told them.

"Barak! It is distressing to hear this from you. You have been listening to the Israeli mongrels again. You should know better than that. I've told you before, Barak, that our atomic facilities are engaged in peaceful nuclear energy research."

"My information is that you've shipped three nuclear bombs outside Iran."

Ahmanutjob froze again. It was impossible that this infidel should have such top-secret information.

"Bombs? There are no bombs, my friend," Mahmoud said. "We have no need of them. It is illegal and against our religion to possess such bombs. The Jews are lying to you again, Barak. We have no bombs."

"You've got three of them."

"No. No bombs," Ahmanutjob said. "I swear on my mother's grave that we have no bombs. You tell your Jewish friends we have no bombs. They won't believe you, of course. But you should tell them there is nothing to worry about. But *we* are worried about American naval movements near the Strait of Hormuz. You have the John C. Stennis carrier group lurking in our coastal waters. Why is that? Are you trying to start a war with us? Are you planning to attack the Islamic Republic of Iran?"

"No, Mahmoud," Omeba replied quickly. "We're not trying to start anything."

"You have imposed economic sanctions on us," Mahmoud countered. "That is not very friendly. That in itself is an act of war. Perhaps I will shut down the Strait of Hormuz and see how you like the West getting its oil supplies shut off. You will get blamed for it you know. The French will call you first, then the Germans, and then the International Herald Tribune. You will be blamed. How is your re-election going?"

"No bombs?" Omeba replied. "Are you sure?"

"I promise you. On my father's life. We have no bombs. We are a peaceful nation. But we will fight you if you bring that aircraft carrier of yours any further into the Persian Gulf. I have forty submarines and hundreds of ships ready to swarm your fleet. And we can shoot your ships from our shores. We have excellent artillery and smart missiles. I think we had better shut down the waterway anyway, just to show you and the Europeans that we can do it."

Ahmanutjob gave his aide a leering grin, which was greeted in return with a hysterically clownish facial contortion. Ahmanutjob put his hand over the phone and doubled over in laughter. It took him a full minute to compose himself and bring the receiver back to his ear. Omeba was droning on about something.

"....so if I agree to stop all current military operations in the Gulf will you agree to retrieve your bombs?"

"All military operations you say?" Mahmoud asked. He wondered how much he had missed. He could not believe his luck. The carrier group had been driving his military commanders insane for days. "You will stop *all* military operations in the Persian Gulf? Do you mean that?"

"Of course I mean it," Omeba promised. "I've given you my thinking on this important matter over the last couple of minutes, and I'm sure you will agree that there is nothing to gain by any more violence in the Middle East. I'm willing to take the first step for peace. Just like I'm doing with Russia."

"Are you really going to reduce your nuclear stockpile by seventy percent? For nothing in return from the Russians? I heard about that but no one believes it."

"Believe it," Omeba said. "More than that, we're giving the Russians our top nuclear secrets as an additional gesture of good faith. I'm willing to go the extra mile with the Islamic Republic of Iran as well. As I just said, I'll issue the executive order to stop all American and allied military operations in the Persian Gulf, if you'll agree to retrieve your nuclear bombs and put them somewhere the news media can't find them."

"You are serious?"

"I'm serious," Omeba said. "I just want the world to be a safer place. I believe that if world leaders talked more, then there would be less misunderstanding and bloodshed. Do we have a deal?"

"But we have no nuclear bombs," Ahmanutjob replied.

"If you did have any nukes, would we have a deal?"

"Why...yes!" Mahmoud could not believe what was happening. It was like a dream. Allah be praised! "If you will shut down all American and allied military operations, and move your aircraft carrier battle group out of the Persian Gulf, then we do have a deal. Yes, we do. Indeed. Yes."

"You'll get the bombs?"

"If we have any bombs we will get them and bring them back onto Iranian soil where no one can see them."

"I have your word on this?"

"I give you my word. On the beard of the Prophet. You have my solemn word."

"Good then," Omeba said. "Thank you, Mahmoud, for helping me clear up this little misunderstanding. I'll sign the executive order immediately. As-salaam, Mahmoud."

"Wa 'alaykum salaam, my friend," Ahmanutjob replied. "It is good to have a friend like you."

He put the phone on the cradle on his desk and stared at it. He could not believe what had just happened. Mahmoud was furious that the Americans knew about the three Torches of Jihad. The Israelis were sure to know more. Much more. That could be a problem. But nonetheless, a miracle had just happened.

The nuclear weapons had to be protected at all costs. Everything depended on them. If the Americans actually did stop all military operations in the Persian Gulf, then that might make it possible to sneak the Torches of Jihad out of the region and get them to their targets. He only needed a week to get the bombs into position: two or three weeks at most. Nuclear jihad was imminent. Perhaps he could get the President of the United States to help him further. This was worth thinking about.

"Did you lie to the infidel, Mahmoud?" his aide asked, stifling a grin.

"How does a believer lie to an infidel?" Ahmanutjob replied. "It is impossible. Can you lie to a dog?"

5

THE PARTY LINE

President Omeba didn't enjoy the weekly Cabinet Meetings as much as he used to. At first they were fun: everyone shut up and rapturously listened to his brilliant ideas and florid ruminations, which were all rooted in standard socialist agitprop — the requisite provender for all American ivy league universities. Everyone in the room understood him perfectly; all of the Cabinet members were highly educated, red diaper babies. No new thinking or ideas ever cluttered their discussions.

But after three years of chaotic, roller coaster governance — the steepest presidential learning curve in American history — it had become abundantly clear why nothing they tried was working. The administration consistently pulled its policies and reforms from the socialist handbook. These policies proved ruinous to the economy, its national security, foreign relations, national health, unemployment and the food and energy supplies. Not one sector of the national economy escaped grievous damage from the socialist reform programs. Omeba administration policies just didn't work for America.

Quite a number of Americans were getting roundly pissed off about the *new* problem in Washington: the Omeba administration. Worse, the liberal base had lost enthusiasm for the hope and change that was promised them. Whatever hope and change was *supposed* to be, it never materialized to their satisfaction. Many of them lost faith in Barak Hussein Omeba. This presented a severe crisis for Omeba's re-election prospects.

The Omeba administration was forced to make cosmetic changes in the way it appeared to govern. Appearance was everything. Appearance meant more than substance. Omeba's government had to *appear* to move toward the center to re-attract the swing vote. So they focused efforts on the appearance of movement to the center. This tactic largely worked, and many of the swing voters swung back into the Omeba camp. But the administration knew that it still had a serious voter gap, and if re-election was to remain a viable prospect, they had to quickly change the way the administration was perceived by the American people. Appearance was everything. Appearance was political reality.

The Cabinet meeting promised to be an interesting one. Rahm Adramelech, the President's Chief of Staff and Valerie Garrotte, Special Advisor to the President, had decided on a new course of action for the administration.

In addition to Cabinet Officers, the Cabinet Room was stuffed with federal executive department heads. Omeba sat in the middle of the table, with the Vice President, Joe Bidet, sitting to his right. Rahm Adramelech sat at the far end of the table.

Rahm was known as "The Godfather" because of his Chicago mob connections and shady way of doing things. He was the administration's top *Consigliere*. He advised the President and got things done for him. He made offers people dare not refuse. He wielded his power ruthlessly, the Chicago way. Nobody screwed with Rahm.

Valerie Garrotte sat at the opposite head of the table from Rahm. Valerie was Omeba's closest friend and confidant. They went back a long way: from running in the Chicago political rackets together, to his various campaigns, and now finally, all the way to the White House. She had advised and comforted him every step of the way. They were very close. Moochelle thought they were too close.

To Omeba's immediate right was Secretary of State, Hillary Clitman. Omeba gave her that position to shut her up and keep her too busy to challenge him during re-election. Bidet had become a liability, so Omeba's plan was for Bidet and Hillary to switch jobs during the next election cycle. He liked to keep his friends close and his enemies closer.

The Attorney General, Eric Holdup, pondered a large stack of documents on the table in front of him. He was entertaining the notion of testifying before Congress the following day that he had not read the documents and had no knowledge of them.

The Secretary of Defense, Leon Panera, a lifelong Democratic Party political hack, was just settling into his latest role in government. Last week he had been the Director of the CIA. This week he was Secretary of Defense. His qualifications for both positions were his degrees in political science and law, and strong political connections in the Democratic Party.

The Secretary of the Treasury, Timothy Geitmare, fiddled incessantly with his fountain pen; writing numbers on his legal pad and on his shirt cuff. He wrote numbers on everything. The Secretary of Homeland Defense, Janet Napolitburo, sat quietly, carefully watching everyone in the room. She had learned that true national security did not consist of defending the people from outside aggression; it depended on monitoring and controlling the actions and movements of the citizens — all of them, including Cabinet Members.

The large oval table was littered with notebooks, glasses of water and cups of coffee. The walls were lined with chairs filled with aides whispering to one another, taking notes and trying to look important.

Portraits of George Washington and Franklin Delano Roosevelt loomed over the Cabinet Room proceedings. Rahm looked coldly around the room. He took his spoon and rapped his glass. The insistent tinking broke through the chatter and instantly stopped all conversation. The Cabinet meeting was in session.

"Thank you all for coming today," Rahm said. "The meeting will be brief. As you know, these meetings have had a lot of protracted discussion lately. But no results. I know that many of you have ideas you think are valuable, but instead of getting your input today, we're just going to solve the problems on the table without discussion from any of you. The President has an opening remark."

President Omeba didn't waste any time.

"These meetings aren't producing the results we need," he said to them. "There needs to be more inspiration here! We need more moon shot!"

The Cabinet Members looked at one another. Rahm had just told them to keep their mouths shut. The President was asking for moon shot.

"Let's cut to the chase and save each other a lot of time," the President said. "I know more about policies on any particular issue than my policy directors. I know exactly what needs to be done for every problem we face. What I need you people to do is implement my policies. I don't need you to think — and I certainly don't need your advice on anything. Your job is to take my words and make them reality. That hasn't been happening."

The Cabinet Members were stunned. Some hung their mouths open. President Omeba took their dumbfounded expressions as an indication that they needed more instruction to get them properly oriented. He continued.

"Tim," he said, turning to the Treasury Secretary, Tim Geightmare. "Do you know why the two stimulus spending packages didn't work? We spent nearly five trillion dollars to jump-start the American economy, yet after spending all that money the unemployment rate has increased and the economy has gotten worse. Do you know why that is?"

Geightmare felt sure this was a trick question. Everyone knew why government spending didn't work. It never worked. It had taken him three years in government as Treasury Secretary to discover that everything he learned at Dartmouth and Johns Hopkins about Keynesian economics was wrong.

"Well, sir. We didn't actually spend the entire five trillion on stimulating the economy. About half of it went to reward our political supporters and pour money into green energy programs. The other half went down the Wall Street rat hole to the banks and insurance companies. We didn't expect a return on the political money, and most of the green energy money went to China. The money that went to the financial institutions was paid out in bonuses and the rest just disappeared. There's no payback there either."

"You're missing the point, Tim, and that's why I called on you first. I can always count on you to do that. You're a Keynesian economist, Tim. You should know the answer to this. The idea is that we pour massive amounts of tax money into the government to stimulate the economy. But it didn't work. What happened?"

Geitmare squirmed in his chair. He preferred working from his dark cell deep in the bowels of the Treasury Department. He hated meetings like this. Instead of writing numbers on everything, he was expected to actually produce something. It wasn't fair. They didn't like him. Nobody liked him. Nobody had ever liked him, not even his mother. And now he was getting picked on again. But he did have an answer for the President.

"What happened?" Geightmare repeated. "Well, sir. Since you took office, unemployment went from 7.6% to 9.1% — officially. We're not going to budge off that number — at least not officially. Realistically, unemployment is at 16.2% overall. Only 67% of American men have jobs now. Black unemployment is at 50%. Since the stimulus packages, we've seen food prices increase 29%, gasoline prices have doubled and housing foreclosures have increased by a factor of twenty..."

"That's my point!" President Omeba shouted, slamming his hand on the table. The Cabinet Members jerked to attention. Nobody got the President's point.

"That is exactly my point! We spent five trillion dollars to stimulate the economy just enough to ensure my reelection — and what happened? The opposite of what we wanted! *Why is that?* Is it because my economic policies have not been implemented?"

"Actually, sir," Geitmare replied. "The administration's economic policies *have* been implemented to a large degree. This is what happens when you force socialist economic policies on a capitalist economy. It forces the capitalist economy to collapse. We've seen it happen. We *made* it happen."

"Look...government spending is supposed to boost the economy," Omeba replied, "at least for a little while. George Maynard Keynes says so. But I want to know why the five trillion stimulus dollars we pumped into the economy only made it worse. Have you seen my approval ratings?" Omeba asked, exasperated. He shot his hands up in mock surrender.

"Mr. President," Geitmare replied, "we *have* succeeded in the first phase of implementing a socialist economy. Socialist economies consume money like a black hole consumes light. The stimulus trillions were sucked down the black hole of our socialist economy. Your policies were designed to give America a socialist economy — right? Well, sir, that's been a raging success. We pretty much have a socialist economy now. All of the economic indicators and numbers prove it. Our unemployment numbers are way up, housing prices and cost of goods are approaching those of socialist economies, and our currency valuation is in free fall. By any reasonable measure, your transformation of the economy to a socialist model has been a raging success."

"Oh..." the President said. He leaned back in his chair to ponder this message. "Well, maybe things aren't so bad after all. What's the forecast, Tim?"

"The American economy is going over a cliff, sir," he replied, relieved that the President saw his point. "Congress is *not* going to cut spending — not as long as Democrats hold the Senate and Red Harry is in charge. But China has signaled that they're going to stop lending us money to pay interest on the debt we've already acquired."

"So what do we do?"

"We monetize the debt."

The President gave Geightmare a blank stare.

Rahm Adramelech leaned forward to whisper into the President's ear. "We *print* more *money.*"

"Won't that lead to inflation?" the President asked.

"Sure," Geightmare replied. "Big time. We'll be at twelve percent inside eighteen months, but we really need to do it. Since you took office the value of the dollar has dropped seventeen percent.

This will help us explain it and get dollar devaluation to a nice even number — say forty percent. I'm pretty sure the media won't ask too many questions. They haven't touched the economy so far."

The President considered what he'd just been told. Geightmare had just given him an idea. He got a faraway look as he thought out loud.

"You know," he said dreamily. "I don't know why we didn't think of this before. If the Chinese won't lend us any more money to pay the interest on the debt, then why don't we just *print* what we need? Why don't we just print enough money to pay off the national debt entirely?"

The Cabinet Members cast worried looks at one another, but nobody said anything. They'd had three years of hair-brained schemes like this one to deal with.

"See?" President Omeba declared. "I'm a genius! I've just solved all of the economic problems we're facing. But I know there's more to it. And I think Tim is on to something else that's very important here: We've established that *my* economic policies have *not* failed. The problem is that my staff and Cabinet members have failed to communicate this message properly. Where's Gay? Where's my Press Secretary?"

"Yessir?" Gay Corney said, from a chair along the wall.

"We've got to get this message out right away," the President decreed. "Rahm? I need a memo to all Secretaries and Department heads: The economy is on track and in sync with our economic policies. Everything is good. Gay, I want a press release right away. The economy is good. Don't take any questions. Just say that it's taking longer than we thought because of legacy problems from the Boosh administration."

"Yessir," Gay said. "The economy is good. The President's policies are working. It's Boosh's fault. We own the economy. It's good. Got it."

"That's good," Omeba said. "I like that. And give them some statistics to back it up: something to prove that our government programs are working. And, Gay, tell them to keep drilling that message into the American people."

"Yes sir."

Tim Geightmare offered a few suggestions. "You could tell the public that the most essential government programs are highly successful and doing better than ever these days. The welfare rolls have tripled in the last three years — three hundred percent growth! Food stamp participation has increased sixty percent. Forty-seven percent of the population, or nearly twenty-one million American families, now depend on food stamps. There has been tremendous growth in these programs."

"It's true," Kathleen Cerberus, the Secretary of Health and Human Services said, looking smug. "Our department has grown more than any other. In 1965, when Lamedim Braines Johnson launched the Great Society, the budget of the entire Unites States was only one hundred and eighteen billion dollars. Today, the HHS alone will spend nine hundred and ten billion dollars. Our social welfare programs are growing very successfully."

The other Cabinet Members looked enviously at Secretary Cerberus. President Omeba was delighted that this aspect of the Cloward-Piven strategy was working so well.

"See there?" Omeba said. "We have lots of government economic programs that are working better than ever. Get that out to the media. And Gay, you tell the networks that the new party line is that the economy is *good*. In fact, it's better than ever. You tell the media that they've been slack on this message and it's costing us."

"Yessir. Will do. We'll start a media campaign immediately. The public will soon know that the Omeba administration's economic policies are a fantastic success and the economy is performing brilliantly for all our supporters."

"Hold it," Geightmare objected. "That might be going *too* far. You can't make a Potemkin Village out of the economy. Sooner or later people are going to notice they don't have jobs and can't afford things."

The Cabinet looked to Omeba for an answer. The President looked calmly at Tim Geightmare and spoke.

"You're forgetting three things," he said. "First, we have *me*. I'll give speeches and press conferences. The public will hear my voice."

Geightmare nodded at this. The power of President Omeba's voice was legend.

"The second thing is that we *own* the news media," the President continued. "They'll do whatever we tell them to do. They'll cover for us. The third thing is that the Democratic Party will get lock step in behind us on this. I'll personally call Red Harry and San Fran Nan. The party apparatchik will spread the word that we live in a fantastic economy. They will issue hundreds of press conferences and spawn thousands of news articles across the nation. There will be no dissent. We will tolerate no intellectual diversity on this matter. This will be the party line."

Murmurs of approval arose from around the conference table.

The new party line had been birthed: The Omeba administration had saved the economy from a deep depression created by the previous Republican administration. The economic renaissance was a miracle. And it was all due to the genius and enormous success of Omeba's fabulous economic programs and policies.

Everyone knew the propaganda campaign would work. The Congressional Democrats were in lock step with the administration. They had to be in order to save the party from a landslide defeat in the next election. The news media would do anything for Omeba. Ideological fidelity with the mainstream media had assured political power for the Democratic Party for over fifty years.

But the political tide and public sentiment had turned against the administration and the media lately. The Democrats and the media knew they had to stand together and bull it through, or they would hang separately. A unified front on economic news was a necessity for them both.

It was a simple matter for the media to convince the people that they lived in a robust successful economy. They merely had to tell the lie repeatedly — every evening on the national news programs. To the Democratic Party/Mainstream Media cabal, the manipulation of public opinion had become routine. They had ongoing media propaganda programs in place for global warming and carbon taxes; green energy and jobs; immigration reform leading to amnesty and open borders; and for a host of other big government spending programs. Adding one more propaganda campaign to the nightly lineup would be easy for them.

The Cabinet members were confident of success. After all, this would merely be the latest deception in a long series that the American people had swallowed whole and believed completely.

And they had their secret weapon: President Omeba was a charismatic leader who held power over millions of union members, government employees and progressive zombies. Omeba was the absolute master of the use of oratory to manipulate the liberal groupmind. Convincing the American sheeple that they lived in a worker's paradise would be a piece of cake for him. He had only to speak, and they would follow.

6

COLONEL JOEL PLUMMER

C olonel Joel Plummer fought to keep his seat in the Special
Forces stealth helicopter. The aircraft bounced and swayed
as gusts of hot air rose in waves from the floor of the Sinai Peninsula.
Seal Team Six favored these specialized helicopters for their range
and stealth, but they were not the most comfortable ride. They flew
west over the Arabian desert toward Egypt.

Colonel Plummer hunted two Iranian supertankers, which he
suspected might be carrying nuclear bombs. At least one of those
weapons was addressed to the USA. On the other side of the Persian
Gulf, the CIA was tracking a group of Iranian oil tankers steaming
in the opposite direction, toward the Strait of Hormuz. CIA
intelligence sources reported that one of those freighters might
be carrying Persian bombs. Those supertankers would never make
it past the US Navy blockade waiting for them. This, of course,
would start a shooting war with Iran. The Iranian government had
dispatched over two hundred military and commercial vessels
towards Hormuz. The military confrontation was only hours away.

But Colonel Plummer had good reason to believe that the tankers headed for the Hormuz Strait were decoys. Plummer's military intelligence was coming from the Israeli Defense Force military intelligence directorate, and from the legendary Mossad. He had a good reliable contact inside Mossad, and Plummer trusted the Israeli information over that of the CIA or Army Intelligence. The Israelis thought the bombs were likely headed in the opposite direction: for Suez — not Hormuz. So Plummer took his Joint SpecOps team to Suez.

Plummer had a force of two hundred and thirty Special Operations commandos following behind him in twenty helicopters. The core of his commando force was Seal Team Six, the fabled blackops warriors. Their mission was to intercept the Suez Canal-bound supertankers and search them. Plummer would be assisted by a small detachment of Mossad Special Forces troops participating in the joint military operation. The Israeli commandos were also airborne and would meet up with Plummer's team at any moment. The SpecOps forces were only minutes from visual contact with the Iranian oil tankers.

They flew over the Sinai Peninsula in a straight vector for the canal. The SpecOps force was engaged in a highly illegal military intrusion into Egyptian air space, in order to attack Iranian-flagged commercial vessels. The commando raid was going to occur in Egyptian waters, inside Egypt's most important commercial asset. The Iranians were sure to see this as an act of piracy and war. The Egyptian government would be furious over the incursion, which they would properly view as a hostile military attack on their sovereign territory. Plummer was expecting a fight.

The American military was determined to intercept the Iranian nukes in the Persian Gulf. Once out into international waters, or on the European continent, finding and neutralizing the bombs would be much harder, if not impossible. The USS Spruance, a guided missile destroyer, was assigned to support the mission. The battleship was stationed in the Mediterranean Sea off Port Said, about one hundred and twenty miles north of the target supertankers.

The destroyer was tasked to fire cruise missiles on the canal locks to close the canal at Port Said, on the Mediterranean side of the canal — *if* Colonel Plummer ordered the strike. The ship was also tasked to destroy the Iranian supertankers, *if* Plummer decided that was needed. It was a high stakes mission, and it revealed the Pentagon's determination to keep nuclear conflagration away from American soil.

But the American civilian government also had its hand in the game. Before Colonel Plummer left the CIA command center in the Negev Desert, he was advised that the White House was considering a hold on certain military actions already under way. This put all of the Operation Persian Bomb military actions in jeopardy, including his own. Commando teams were actively engaged in a dozen separate missions throughout the Middle East, including a major support effort for the Israeli attack on the Bekkah Valley nuke.

Instead of waiting for clarification or further orders, Colonel Plummer launched his commando force. He couldn't wait for the White House to make up its mind about something it knew nothing about, and he was concerned that someone from the State Department might intervene for some arcane diplomatic reason.

The Sinai Peninsula was a gigantic stretch of barren desert between Egypt and Israel. The peninsula shoreline was a rocky wasteland, with thin strips of parched white sand lining the Red Sea. It was dotted with petroleum terminals but little else. Somewhere down below was the place where Moses led the Hebrews out of Egyptian bondage and eventually to the Promised Land. There had been war ever since.

The peninsula served as the essential buffer between Egypt and Israel. Both sides constantly watched the borders. The Egyptians monitored the border for smugglers. The Israelis monitored the border for terrorist infiltration or the massing of Egyptian troops, such as the one that triggered the 1967 Arab-Israeli Six Day War.

The line of helicopters left the Sinai Peninsula and flew over the vast waters of the Red Sea. Colonel Plummer's headset beeped. The helicopter pilot told him that the city perched at the mouth of the canal was Suez. There was a little greenery along the western shore of the canal. The huge desalination plants along the shore made enough fresh water to sustain a thin green swath of agriculture, which reached far north into the Nile Delta.

Colonel Plummer's headset beeped again. It was his Mossad contact, Moshe Argaman. Moshe had operational military intelligence to share: There were nine oil tankers and sixteen freighters in the canal. The two Iranian vessels they sought had already entered the canal, and were at the first turn at Fayed. They would be swooping down on the tankers in less than two minutes.

A large Egyptian air force base and military city was situated at Kibrit, which the tankers had passed only an hour before. The Egyptian military would have helicopters and patrol boats headed their way in short order. It would take time to search the tankers; so they made arrangements to deal with the Egyptian military when it arrived. It couldn't be helped. The entire Egyptian military network would be on high alert at any moment, if it weren't already. Things were going to get interesting in the next few minutes.

Plummer relayed Argaman's information to his SpecOps commanders trailing behind. The plan was for the SpecOps teams to swoop down on the supertankers, combat assault, and commandeer them. Plummer ordered that the tankers be run aground on the eastern shore, on the opposite side of the waterway from Egyptian military assets and the small regional municipalities. The Mossad translators and commandos would arrive in the vanguard of the assault. The combined teams would begin searching the tankers immediately, using Geiger counters and ionizing particle detectors. If the nuclear bombs were on board the tankers, they would find them. That didn't mean the bombs would be easy to recover, however. At an estimated 2,400 pounds each, the job of retrieving the nukes would be a demanding one. But the SpecOps warriors were prepared, versatile and cunning: they would figure a way if it could be done.

If Plummer could not extract the nukes, he would destroy the tankers and bombs in place using cruise missiles launched by the U.S.S. Spruance. That would make a mess of metal to sort through, and the resulting explosion and inferno would likely render any nuclear device inoperable. If the bombs *were* on the tankers, the US Navy might even be allowed to recover them from the tanker wreckage at a later date.

Desert heat blasted through the open window of the SpecOps helicopter. Plummer could see the Mossad helicopters crossing the peninsula, converging with them on the two Iranian oil tankers below. The vessels were enormous. They were Very Large Crude Carrier tankers, each three hundred meters in length. Both hung low in the water, moving at a snail's pace. Fully loaded VLCC's had tremendous inertia and could take fifteen minutes to stop under full emergency power. Plummer planned to use that inertia to drive the tankers to the far shore.

He estimated that commando mission time on the tankers would be one to two hours. It could take longer. He expected a visit from Egyptian helicopters within thirty minutes to an hour of touchdown. Their jets would not be far behind. If Plummer's team could not find the nukes quickly, or if his men came under oppressive fire, then he would order cruise missile strikes from the U.S.S. Spruance, and make his escape.

Plummer was grateful for the Israeli intelligence and for their commandos and helicopter support on this mission. He knew their assistance in locating the nukes could be invaluable. The Mossad had a way of extracting information from Arabs and he welcomed their help.

His targets loomed just ahead and below. The teams had been briefed and knew what to do. His officers had planned well. Colonel Plummer gave the signal to go hot.

His helicopter dove like a dragonfly, followed by a score of specially configured and heavily armed Blackhawk and Chinook helicopters. They plummeted down to the gigantic supertankers like a swarm of black hornets, each pilot sizing up possible landing sites. Plummer's pilot picked a landing area in front of the bridge and threaded a path to an area relatively clear of the spaghettiwork piping and equipment. They bounced to a halt. Half a dozen other helicopters landed just outside their rotorwash. Seal Team Six warriors poured out of the helicopters and combat assaulted the supertanker.

The commandos swarmed the bridge. Plummer ran to the steel stairway beneath the bridge and hunkered under it. The Iranian crew had locked the watertight doors and the Seals had to set C-4 breaching charges on them. He knelt down for a moment to radio his second in command, Captain Laker. Laker's team was assaulting the other petroleum supertanker. A change in the noise level caused him to look up. The Israeli helicopters veered away from their approach vector and turned back to the Sinai Peninsula. He was astonished, dumfounded.

His headset beeped. It was Moshe Argaman, his Mossad contact.

"Colonel, my friend," the Israeli greeted. "I am sorry to be leaving you in your moment of need, but we have been recalled."

"What?" Colonel Plummer couldn't believe his ears. "We're in the middle of a combat mission! You can't quit on us now. We need you. We *desperately* need you!"

"It can't be helped, Colonel," the Israeli officer commiserated. "We have been officially ordered to abort our support mission. It seems that your President Omeba has pulled American support for our mission in the Bekkah Valley. The satellite imagery has been shut off and your combat assets and troops have been withdrawn. We received no explanation as to why. But my superiors have recalled our team in retaliation. I am sorry my friend. I truly am."

Colonel Plummer sank to the deckplate. SpecOps commandos rushed past him, intent on the mission at hand. There was an explosion, then shooting. The Navy Seals took the bridge.

"Moshe, listen to me," Plummer said. "Let me call my command and see what's happening. I need you down here. I need you to help me find the package."

"I am truly sorry, Colonel. Our mission is aborted by IDF command. I must obey orders. Good luck to you."

Plummer watched as the Israeli jet helicopters flew rapidly away, back across the Sinai Peninsula, back home to The Promised Land. It was a crushing tactical loss.

But he still had a mission. Plummer keyed his headset and called the U.S.S. Spruance missile ship standing off Port Said in the Mediterranean. His encoded call was transmitted directly to the Captain.

"Captain, I may need your missiles pretty quick. We've had some changes here. Are you tracking the targets?"

"Sorry, Colonel. Our support mission was just terminated. We cannot provide the ordinance on target or complete *any* part of the combat plan."

"Do you recall the *nature* of our mission, Captain?" Colonel Plummer asked, incredulous at what was happening.

"I do indeed, Colonel. These orders came code red directly from the Pentagon. My ship is standing down. Do not attempt any more radio communication. Good luck."

Plummer called his command center in the Negev Desert and spoke with his CIA counterpart, who claimed to know nothing about the mission aborts by the Israelis and the United States Navy. He promised to get back to Colonel Plummer.

Plummer rose, wiped crude oil from his hands onto his fatigue pants and looked up at the bridge. A Seal waved down at him. They had at most an hour to search both tankers, find the nuke or nukes, and rig them for removal. He was on his own. He knew that they would have to fight their way out of Egypt and back to Israel. His mission had been compromised — by the *White House*. Colonel Plummer wondered how many American soldiers Barak Hussein Omeba was going to get killed before he was out of office.

7

THE OVAL OFFICE

President Omeba tiptoed down the stairs from the third floor to the ground floor. He slept in the President's Bedroom — *she* in the Queen's Room. Occasionally he could sneak out of the Executive Residence and avoid her entirely. He passed by the elevators because she could hear them and quickly be onto him. She was fast for one so large.

He peeped out of the stairwell on the west side of the Residence. A Secret Service guard pretended not to notice him. Omeba whispered to him.

"Pssst. Have you seen the Wookie?"

The guard looked at him.

"The Wookie! Have you seen her?" Omeba demanded.

The guard shook his head.

Omeba emerged from the stairwell, tiptoed into the West Colonnade and went outside. It was cool in the morning air. Clouds threatened rain later in the day. He entered the West Wing a minute later, breathing easier. The coast was clear. He might be able to get in a day of work without even seeing Moochelle. Once inside the Oval Office he could barricade himself behind aides and secretaries. He would be safe.

Secret Service guards greeted him with nods and 'Morning, Mr. President.' He waved them away as if they were gnats. He walked through the hallway and past the Cabinet Room. His secretary wasn't in yet. Normally, Omeba wouldn't be in the office until after ten, but he didn't sleep well last night.

The Persian Bomb thing frightened him silly. He had a bad dream about it last night. If a nuke actually went off in the United States, then his reelection was sunk. But fortunately, the diplomatic understanding he'd reached with Mahmoud Ahmanutjob took care of the problem of the wandering nuclear bombs. Barak told himself he had bigger problems to face that day.

The constant public protests against his policies and programs were starting to alarm him. He had a tin ear as far as customary protests from ordinary citizens were concerned. But the recent protests had grown so large and noisy that he could no longer ignore them. Even the media were starting to report on the protests and give semi-accurate estimates of crowd sizes. The crowds were monstrously large, clamorous and, worst of all, visible to the media. They could no longer be dismissed.

A genuine grass-roots political movement — The Tea Party — had sprung up in the wake of the passage of OmebaCare and the trillions of dollars lost to the stimulus spending. Despite media characterizations of the Tea Partiers as racist rednecks, the movement continued to grow. Thousands of blacks joined the Tea Party, as well as Asians and Hispanics. The Tea Partiers even offered up a black presidential candidate to run against him in the next election.

That was a nightmare. The Tea Party represented a very real threat to his Presidency.

And a new group had sprung up, calling its members The Patriots. They had no political affiliation and no leaders, but there were millions of them. They were a complete mystery to Omeba.

Omeba crept into the Oval Office. He had redone the décor and colors to give it a more African flavor, but had to admit that it looked bland in comparison to the George Boosh colors. The Oval Office looked like the camping section in an Eddie Bauer catalog. The President of Zimbabwe had similar office colors, only his office looked better.

Omeba strode to the Resolute Desk — the desk that Ronald Regal, Bill Clitman and the Booshes used to steer the nation. It was the most powerful desk in the world. He was half way across the office when he heard the screech he dreaded most.

"*BARRY HUSSEIN!*" the First Lady screamed.

His heart skipped a beat. He automatically raised his hands to protect his head from the clawed smack he knew was coming. It was the Wookie. He was doomed.

"Oh! Moochelle," he cried. "You startled me."

"I'll startle yo' ass, Barry," she yelled. "What you doin' sneaking around the White House like this anyway? You look like a *fool*, Barry."

"Yes, Dear."

"I oughta smack you *silly* for makin' me wait here all morning for you. Straighten your narrow ass up now. I gotta talk to you."

"Yes, Dear."

"Our law licenses..."

"What?"

"Our law licenses..."

"But Moochelle, dear...we surrendered them to the Illinois bar to avoid the investigations and disbarment petitions. You know that."

"I want mine back. I want my law license back right now," she said. "I figger you might not get reelected and I want my license to practice law back. We can get it now. You just write a letter on White House letterhead and the bar will give us our licenses back. You also tell 'em to stop those silly investigations too. Get the FBI to investigate whoever is investigating us. Tell 'em we have a file on they asses."

"Honey, I can't," Omeba objected. "It's part of the plea deal. Blago took the fall, but he went down swinging. He struck a deal with the SIEU and the Mafia, then he short-changed the judge. I had to make up the difference. The whole thing's a mess. The judge wanted our licenses and a favor to close the investigation and seal the records. He's a *Chicago* judge. I still *owe* him that favor. We can't open that can of worms right now, Moochelle. It would blow up in our faces."

She spun angrily on him. He cringed.

"I don't give a whoop!" Moochelle barked. "Fix the judge! You're good at that. Fix the damn Chicago judge and get me my license back. You got two weeks, Barry."

"Or what?"

"Or I tell Joseph Fairman at *World Net Daily* what he desperately wants to know."

"You wouldn't do *that*!" Omeba cried. "That would bring down our Presidency. He and The Donald are the only ones in the country with balls enough to pursue this birther thing. You'll burn with me, Moochelle!"

"My law license, Barry," she snapped, walking toward the door. "Or I go nuclear. You don't wannna see me angry, Barry."

"Okay, Moochelle. I'll get your license back somehow. I'll think of something."

"Good boy."

She left the Oval Office. Barry walked to the Resolute Desk and put his head down on it for a few moments. He looked up to make sure Moochelle was truly gone. He covered his head with his hands. He had a pounding headache. It was a Moochelle headache, which was the worst kind. They usually turned into tooth-cracking migraines. Valerie was the only one who could rub them out. He closed his eyes. People would be coming into the office soon to work. It was going to be a long day.

The President of the United States awoke to a discreet rapping on the desk. He snorted awake and looked bleary-eyed at his Chief of Staff.

"Oh. Hi, Rahm. I must have dozed off."

"Hi, Barry. Time to get going. You have a busy day today. I've got a raft of bills I need you to sign into law and we have an important meeting with Eric."

"Another meeting with the Attorney General? So soon?" Omeba complained. "It seems like we're meeting with him every other day."

"Mr. *President*," Rahm chided. "We talked about this. You can't make a socialist omelet without breaking a few capitalist eggs. We are *going* to have problems with the Constitution and the law. It's part of the game. Eric Holdup can get us through the legal hoops."

"Oh all right. What's up first?"

Rahm Adramelech placed a thick stack of papers on the Resolute Desk. Valerie Garrotte entered with two photographers, who quickly set up their lights and cameras. She gave the President his private wink and smile.

"The first is an executive order to repeal *Don't Ask, Don't Tell*. This will lock in the gay vote for us," Rahm said.

"Well, I'll certainly sign that!" Omeba took his pen and posed it where Rahm indicated. He looked up and smiled at the cameras. "It's time we stopped religious beliefs and cultural values from interfering with the rights of homosexuals."

The photographers clicked merrily away.

"Say..." Omeba said, "Shouldn't we have Elton Jane or Ellen DeGenerate standing behind me when I sign this? We should at least get Chrissy Matthews here to do an interview."

"We'll restage the signing with the GBLT people later. It's all arranged."

"Okay. Say, how's the military taking it? I got a lot of flack about this from the Pentagon and the Joint Chiefs of Staff. The Air Force Academy and West Point raised hell with me. Not too much flak from the Navy. There are a lot of prominent generals and admirals threatening to resign over this."

"Not a problem," Valerie replied. "Like Rahm said, you have to break some capitalist eggs. This is just the beginning. Now we'll demand same-sex military weddings and full military benefits for same-sex spouses. Isn't it romantic?"

"Sure is," Rahm agreed. "And Valerie's right. This is only the beginning. After you sign this order, we'll have to provide separate barracks for transgender soldiers. They refuse to bunk with people of only one gender — unless it's the one they want to have sex with."

"You don't think we can put them in with the lesbians?" Omeba asked. "You'd think that they would *like* that."

"No," Valerie said. "It wouldn't work at all. You can put the homosexuals in with the transgenders, and even some of the trans-sexuals — but not the lesbians. They want to be in with the straight women. No male organs allowed."

"Well then, how about the bisexuals?" Omeba asked. "Surely they wouldn't mind if we put them in with the transgenders."

"I don't know about that," Rahm said. "They might be okay with the transvestites but they might have problems with the transgenders. You know, the hormones and surgery and stuff. They can be pretty bitchy. Bisexuals can be pretty uptight about their issues too. I think we better keep them separate."

"I'm getting confused," President Omeba admitted. "By signing this executive order getting rid of *Don't Ask, Don't Tell,* we're telling the world that we're allowing gays to serve openly in the United States military. We said to ourselves that we were going to make them bunk with the straight males...maybe turn some of them around, and take the macho edge off the military, so to speak. Right now we only have two barracks: one for males and one for females. Their sexual preference shouldn't matter once I sign this order. We should put males with homosexuals and females with lesbians. Are you now telling me that we need to build more barracks to accommodate the transgenders?"

"It's a bit more involved than that," Valerie admitted. "We'll need to have five separate barracks for our new military."

"*Five*? Are you kidding me? That would cost a fortune," Omeba protested.

"They're three percent of the vote, Barry."

"Oh...okay. We'll cancel an aircraft carrier. But why five barracks?"

"You need one for the straight males and the gays, one for straight females and lesbians, one for transgenders — the transsexuals and transvestites, one for the pansexuals and one for the androgynes."

"The *whut*?"

"I know you've got the first three. You've spoken in support of GBLT issues forever. The pansexuals and androgynes are a growing voice, Barry."

"How much of the vote do *they* represent?"

"Less than one thousandth of one percent," Valerie replied. "But they have rights too, Barry. They have a right to serve in the armed forces and shoot guns at people. And that's what they want to do."

"But who *are* they?"

"The pansexuals do any kind of sex: fetishes, pedophilia, bestiality, paraphilia, necrophilia...you get the drift. They do all kinds of sex, so they don't fit in a single box. We need a place for them in the military. You'd be surprised how many people in our party want to have sex with animals. The androgynes don't fit into a box either. They drift in and out of sexual identity...sometimes with no sexual identity at all. They may be male or female-bodied, but their psychological identities are in a state of flux. Sometimes they claim to have no gender. They are gender fluid. They need their own barracks, Barry. You really don't want to put them in with the others."

"Oh. Okay then. They'll all vote for me?"

"You bet. Sign this and you'll own them forever."

"There!" Omeba said, signing the executive order with a flourish. "Now we've got gays in the military."

"Yep," Rahm agreed. "And transsexuals, transvestites, pedophiles, sadomasochists, transgenders, beastophiles, necrophiliacs, androgynes and a dozen other sexual orientations. We just made history. And this is only the beginning."

"But how long do you think it will take to work?"

"You mean to break down order in the military structure?" Valerie asked. She looked to Rahm.

"About five years for a complete breakdown in discipline and military order," Rahm said. "It will have an immediate effect on morale, of course, and that's worth quite a bit. But it'll take longer to really dismantle the core of the military. Hopefully it will happen by the time we need it. We need four more years to help it along... get it entrenched in the military so people get used to the idea. Then we go after the heteronormative society at large. That's where the real social transformation will take place."

Rahm was right. This was only the beginning. Once they used the gays to break down the cultural and religious moral barriers, then they could start working on equal access to religious assets in the military. They would see to it that the Druids, atheists, agnostics, pagans and Satanists all had their own temples and chaplains provided at tax-payer expense. Once they had religious equality in the military — and sidelined Christianity — then they could begin to work on society as a whole.

Omeba envisioned a form of Americans with Religious Disabilities Act — only it would be called the Religious Equality Act. Under the act, he could require that Catholic Hospitals perform abortions, that Baptist churches provide equal worship space with the Church of Satan, that the Church of Christ provide STD counseling for teen homosexuals and the bi-curious. He would see to it that all of the Christian denominations opened up their churches and shared resources with the Pagans, Hindus, Buddhists, Wiccans, Muslims, Zoroastrians and others. He wanted one-stop religious shopping open to all, regardless of denomination or belief system.

Omeba wanted to ensure that everyone would share the religious wealth, instead of it being concentrated with the Catholics and Protestants.

He became giddy thinking about the possibilities. A One World religion was a pet project of his. Once he got God off the greenback and completely out of the schools, and most of the churches, then he would know that his day had arrived.

President Omeba looked up at his fellow travelers. He knew that his team was having a real impact on American society. Just one little policy change like this would have enormous implications for society as a whole. He had three dozen more like it in the works. Before he was through, he'd have hundreds more executive orders and policy changes working their way irrevocably through the foundations and structures of government and society. His presidency was truly going to be transformative.

8

BEYOND THE CONSTITUTION

"Who's next?" President Omeba barked. He'd been working through a long procession of people and agenda items all day. It was time for a mocha.

"The Attorney General, Mr. President," the Chief of Staff replied. "You'll be with him for two full hours today."

"Say that again."

"The Attorney General..."

"No...just the part after that."

"You mean...*Mr. President*?"

"Yeah. Say *that* again. I can't hear it enough."

Rahm Adramelech straightened up and grinned.

"I witness that thought, *Mr. President*. The Attorney General is outside. With your permission, *Mr. President*, I'll buzz him in."

They grinned at each other. Eric Holdup strolled into the Oval Office with half a dozen attorney-aides. Omeba took one look at the group and tilted his head toward the private study next to the Oval Office. The room was small but it was microphone free. He wanted no recordings of this meeting. The study had a kitchenette, a conference table and chairs for eight. It was the famous blowjob room, where Bill Clitman decorated Monica Lewdinski's blue cotton dress with Presidential DNA.

"Eric, you look like you've got quite an agenda today," Omeba observed, eyeing the thick portfolio.

"Yes, Barry. But I'm restricting today's discussion to the Constitutional questions."

"Not again."

"Yes, Judicial Watch has filed another lawsuit. And the Republicans won't shut up either. We've been playing it fast and loose with the Constitution since we've been in office, and some of it is catching up to us. We seem to be able to go around Congress without much of a problem, especially the Senate. But these damn czars of yours are causing all kinds of problems."

"Not the czars again."

"Yep. You've got too many of them. More than any President in history. These people are not approved by the Senate, so anything they do is all your fault."

"Who is it this time?"

"All of them: Car Czar, TARP Czar, Consumer Czar, Green-Jobs Czar, Information Czar, Stimulus Czar, Technology Czar, War Czar, Urban Affairs Czar, Global Warming Czar, Bank Bailout Czar, Sexual Orientation Czar...that's not even a fraction of them. You have got to stop appointing czars, Barry. They have no Constitutional authority to even exist."

"*I* authorized them to exist."

"It's getting out of hand," Holdup said. "When the government took over General Motors and Chrysler...that looked bad. It's fascism — not that there's anything wrong with that — but the public perception of it is bad for us. The conservatives accused us of taking over the auto industry to reward our union supporters, which is exactly what we did. We had to protect their pensions. And when we took over banking and insurance, the Republicans and Tea Partiers accused us of taking over *those* industries too. Their bowels are still in an uproar over that. More fascism. Then we took over the health care industry by forcing OmebaCare down Congress's throat. That's the straw that broke the camel's back. We took over one fifth of the economy. Sixty-six percent of the American people opposed it. Not a single Republican in the House or Senate voted for it. We pushed too far with OmebaCare. It's being challenged in court by twenty-six states and we've got another dozen lawsuits opposing it as well. We're losing too many of the appeals. About half of our Federal judges say OmebaCare is unconstitutional."

"Is it?"

"Only if the Supreme Court says it is. Congress is irrelevant."

Barak Omeba gave Eric Holdup a sour look.

"Look, Eric," he said. "We can't get the stake into the beast's heart without government-provided health care. Once we control health care, then government will control the American people from that day forward. They mess with us...we yank their health care. So you rope-a-dope the states with appeals until the imple-menting programs can get dug in deeper. Once we start paying benefits it'll be too late for *anyone* to stop it."

Attorney General Holder leaned forward and lowered his voice.

"Don't underestimate the Republicans, Barry...or those damned Tea Party activists either. They're coming after us hard on OmebaCare. And they're also chipping away at us on the czars, the Fast and Furious gun control project, Solyndra and all the other green energy investments that turned sour. All the stimulus spending is catching up to us, too. We've got more scandals than I can keep up with. We've got to give them the czars. They're the most expendable. It wouldn't be so bad if the czars weren't wasting so much taxpayer money they have no authority to spend. But they're visible. People are starting to *notice*, Barry."

"Bah! Right wing, flag-waving, racist bigots. Who cares what they think? We have the media."

"It's a grass roots uprising, Barry. Who do you think is outside the White House protesting whenever we do something progressive? It's the American *people*."

"Tea baggers!" Omeba spat. "People who listen to Lush Rimshot. The enemy. There aren't enough of them to matter any more. Haven't you been paying attention? Most people now either work for the government or are dependent on it. We have a hard-core constituency of 35% of the population to oppose the Tea Partiers. That's a rock solid base. We can bring in the swing vote with more government programs and more bold promises — more bread and circuses. That's good for another 15% of the vote. ACORN will continue to work under the radar to round up the illegal alien and dead voters. We'll block the military votes again. Eric, the organizing machine is already in place. We *own* the media. We have everything we need to win an American election. Heck, Eric, all I need to do is give speeches. *I* can bring in the votes all by myself. Yes we can!"

Eric Holdup looked doubtfully at the President.

"The majority of Americans hate us, Barry, and they're coming after us. As your Attorney General I have a duty to tell you that we won't survive the Constitutional challenges facing us."

"You forget that I've just put two Supreme Court judges on the bench — without even a whimper from the Republicans. Both are hard core Marxists. One of them helped me draft OmebaCare.

We're bullet proof. Congress hasn't even got the *cojones* to review the birth certificate."

"Hush!" Attorney General Holdup said. "Don't even talk about *that*. Barry, the Republicans and Tea Baggers hold the House. They're investigating things. Darryl Issawus is breathing down our necks — and don't forget Lush Rimshot. He's worse than a special prosecutor. He's on us like mustard on a Coney Island hot dog. I'm not sure we can hold the news media together either. Remember what they did to Bill Clitman? Jimmuh Carper? They smell blood in the water and they'll come after you too. We can't trust the media. Not really. Every revolution eats its children. You remember that. They'll eat you too, Barry."

"Not me," Omeba said confidently. "The mainstream media believe in me. Heck, Eric, we wouldn't *be* here if it weren't for the mainstream media. The sheeple will suck up everything they say. The media put me in office and they'll keep me here."

"I bet Bill Clitman said the same thing. And he got his butt *impeached*."

Omeba looked at his old friend long and hard.

"But we're talking about me, Eric. I'm not like anybody else. *I'm* in the Oval Office now. This is about what *I* can accomplish for the world. What I am doing now will make the world a better place. I can justify all of the things I'm doing by the results I will obtain. We're going to spread the wealth around, Eric. I can establish the New World Order. I can do this. But I need you to keep the troublemakers and the Constitutionalists off my back while I do the heavy lifting."

"I've got your back, Barry," Eric Holdup said. "But we've got special problems. It's not just the usual suspects: the GOP conservatives, the military, the Christians, the Boy Scouts, small businessmen, working mothers and that whole bunch. It's different now. Now we're facing a groundswell of citizens who want us to stop doing what we're doing. They've got legal resources and the House. They're putting everything we do under a microscope. The Tea Party now has members in Congress and they're ready to go to war. They own a lot of new media and they use it: Briteparts, Lush Rimshot, Han Sanity, Ben Gleck, Laura Smokinham, Philipe Valentino. They've got Fox News. They've got the Family Research Council and a thousand others just like it. They've got huge moneybag bundlers like the Coke Brothers, the Hunter Brothers, the Schwaubs, Templetons, Popes and Camerons. They have all the big industrial corporations, except General Electric. They have the Evangelicals. They own Big Oil. They own the military. Barry, they've got everything they need to come after us — and they *are* fighting back. My people at the FBI have been busy keeping track of their social media, reading email and listening to phone calls. It doesn't look good for us, Barry. There's this new shadow group calling themselves The Patriots. They're springing up everywhere! And I mean in all fifty-seven states!"

"We can fight them, Eric," President Omeba said. "We *have* to if we're going to succeed with our agenda. We've done this before. Put the media on it. Slander their leaders, find their bimbos, play the race card. You know what to do."

"You're not hearing me, Barry. It's more complicated than that," Holdup protested. "It's not just the conservative political party and its media that we have to win against. We don't just have a few big targets to undermine. It's the American people themselves who are our enemy. They have resources the government does not and they're starting to use them. You're underestimating the American people, Barry. That's dangerous."

9

THE JUDAS KISS

Hot roaring wind blasted through the line of SpecOps helicopters fleeing the scene of destruction. The Suez Canal was in flames. Two Iranian VLCC supertankers, each carrying more than eighty million barrels of crude oil burned furiously away inside the Suez Canal.

Colonel Joel Plummer held the battle dressing tight onto the young soldier's neck. He shouted at the medic to come and look, but the medic was waist deep in casualties. Blood was splattered throughout the interior of the throbbing Chinook helicopter. The deck was slippery with it. Casualties had been twenty percent. But they did recover all of the dead. Seal Team Six did not leave its dead behind.

They also recovered one of the Persian bombs. It was slung below the helo in a cargo net. The helicopter could handle the weight, but shrapnel from an Egyptian hellfire missile had damaged the right jet engine. The armored engine compartment was leaking fluids. The good engine could not keep them airborne by itself much longer. They'd thrown out every bit of spare equipment they could to lighten the load. The only dead weight left in the aircraft was the bodies of young American soldiers, and the nuclear bomb slung beneath its belly.

Colonel Plummer had an emergency call into the CIA command post in the Negev Desert. He'd given them his status and pleaded for assistance. The CIA operations chief said he would have to consult higher command to authorize what Plummer requested. He didn't have time for that. If the CIA failed to respond immediately, then his commando team would be forced down in the Sinai Desert on Egyptian soil. Colonel Plummer fully expected that airmobile elements of the Egyptian Second Field Army would be all over them in a matter of minutes. Plummer was determined not to let the Egyptians get their hands on the Persian Bomb. He was equally determined to get the rest of his troops out alive.

They lost only three helicopters. Those went down in the brutal fight to keep Egyptian Navy helicopters from attacking the retreating forces. The balance of his commando team was spread out in the remaining eighteen helos, three of which were trailing smoke. The Chinook pilot shut down the right jet turbine engine. It spun down with a loud, grinding rattle. They would have to set down in a matter of minutes.

The Egyptians would be furious after Suez. They would want revenge. They were coming. Plummer would have to send six of the Blackhawks back to engage the pursuing Egyptian helicopters, while the rest landed and transferred troops to functioning aircraft. They would have to re-rig the nuke under the remaining Chinook. Egyptian jets could be on them at any moment. They had no way to fight them. Too much was happening at once.

Seal Team Six had some luck in the assault on the Iranian VLCCs. They found the nuclear device quickly, using ionizing particle detectors. It was on the lead vessel. The second vessel was clean. The bomb was in a forward hold, submerged under twenty meters of crude oil. The bomb was attached to a cable, and they were able to hook it up to a Chinook and lift it out of the petroleum hold. The bomb had been sealed ingeniously inside a leak proof, steel, shipping container. They lifted the nuke onto the shore where they rigged it to a cargo sling fitted to the heavy Chinook helicopter.

The Navy destroyer he was counting on — the U.S.S. Spruance — had been withdrawn from combat. He had planned to use the cruise missile destroyer's Tomahawk missiles to destroy the VLCC oil tankers and close the Suez Canal. Seal Team Six improvised, using C-4 explosives they attached to the inner and outer hulls.

Colonel Joel Plummer decided that he had to shut down the Suez Canal. If there were truly three Iranian bombs; then he had one of them, the Israelis were after another in the Bekkah Valley, and one was missing. He had no idea where it could be. Nobody had a clue. If it was still in the Persian Gulf, and bound for transit via the Suez Canal, he preferred to trap it in the Gulf if he could. The strategy might buy enough time to find the bomb. And time was in short supply.

His Special Forces commandos cheered loudly when the tankers exploded. The volatile chemical fractions in the crude oil made a spectacular fireball that shot two thousand feet into the air. The secondary explosions broke the keels of both VLCCs and split the double hulls. The tankers burned furiously, emitting a thick black smoke and a flaming oily scum on the water. The Suez Canal was on fire.

The time they had lost rigging the two tankers with explosives was the time the Egyptian army needed to get its own Special Forces commandos in the air and over the lower reaches of the Suez Canal. The Egyptians came on the scene believing that the Israelis were invading Egypt. They came prepared for a hard fight. It was over in ten minutes. Plummer lost forty-six good men and three helicopters. The Egyptians lost eleven helicopters, two light aircraft and over a hundred and twenty men. It was a nasty beginning to a hasty retreat.

Captain Laker's voice came over Plummer's headset, and informed him that four of the damaged helicopters were going to make emergency landings on the At-Tīh Plateau, a broad flat expanse halfway across the Sinai Peninsula. It was time to set Plummer's Chinook down as well. They coordinated plans to pick up the landed troops, bodies and the nuclear device, using the remaining task force helicopters. The commandos would then destroy the abandoned helicopters with explosives.

The emergency operation would put them on the desert plateau for at least thirty minutes. The Egyptians would certainly catch up to them in that time. His team would be exposed to fire from Egyptian helicopters, and perhaps jet aircraft. He didn't expect any of them to survive if the jets showed up.

Joel called the CIA command in the Negev Desert again. It was only one hundred and ten miles away. The CIA Station Commander did not answer the call. *That* message was clear enough: Seal Team Six was disavowed, abandoned. There could be only one reason for this — The White House. Joel had a hard time believing that even President Omeba would do such a thing.

He could bring his troops into the secret CIA base in the Negev without permission. He was sure he could find it again. Or he could look for help elsewhere. He put in an emergency call to Moshe Argaman, his counterpart in the Mossad. Colonel Plummer might be able to get the Mossad to provide him what he needed. He believed he possessed the coin that would interest them. It was dangling in a cargo net beneath his helicopter.

10

COMMANDER IN CHIEF

The Situation Room was a riot of urgent activity. NSC technicians bustled over their computer consoles, bringing in information and images from around the world. Messengers clogged the aisleways, entering and leaving in a continuous stream. Military officers worked through thousands of communiqués in an effort to gain a clearer understanding of what was going on and who was doing what. The information and data coming into the Situation Room made little sense to anyone so far, and the President was due any moment for a briefing. Suddenly the POTUS entered the intelligence center.

President Omeba entered the Situation Room with Valerie Garrotte and Hillary Clitman trailing closely behind. Rahm and Vice President Bidet were already seated at the long mahogany conference table. Janet Napolitburo was also there, having a heated argument with the Secretary of Defense, Leon Panera. Laptops were set up at each chair. General Dimpey stood at the podium. He bent over to receive a whispered, top-secret update from a two-star

General. The wall-sized screens at the end of the Situation Room displayed images from around the world. The room was a scene of organized chaos.

As soon as the President entered, everyone stood and faced him. The military men saluted him. Omeba ignored them all and took his seat at the head of the table. President Omeba had been called to the Situation Room for an emergency briefing. Nobody on his staff could give him any real detail about what was going on. It was a military matter. An NSC Watch Team officer greeted the President and put a sheaf of papers on the desk blotter in front of him. The technician then brought up an image of burning oil tankers on the President's laptop screen. The President looked at the screen and frowned. The flaming hulks were also projected onto the main screens on the far wall.

"What's this all about?" he asked.

"I've got the Iranian supertankers on screen for you, sir," the NSC technician said. "They're in the Suez Canal. We're briefing you on the Persian Bomb crisis, Mr. President."

Omeba gave the technician a nasty look. Then he looked at Rahm.

"National emergency, Mr. President," Rahm said, sliding over to look at the President's screen. It was in the right place: Operation Persian Bomb. He nodded at the President.

Omeba was furious.

"I personally took care of the Persian Bomb thing," Omeba seethed. "I called Ahmanutjob and we worked everything out diplomatically. There is absolutely no need for this kind of military excess." He nodded toward the burning hulks on the screen.

Vice President Bidet and Valerie looked at one another in shock. Rahm spoke up.

"Mr. President, I issued your Executive Order 13666 last night right after we drafted it. We ordered all our military assets in the Persian Gulf to stand down. General Dimpey and I had a rather heated discussion about it last night and another one this morning. The entire Pentagon is raising hell with us about this. General Dimpey called this emergency briefing to bring you up to speed."

Rahm lifted his eyebrow and gave Omeba his stone cold stare, indicating that if General Dimpey didn't start towing the line he'd soon be sleeping with the fishes. Omeba looked at Rahm in frustration and disbelief. Only the military could create a SNAFU of this magnitude. General Dimpey appeared at the podium, turned on his microphone and tapped it. Everyone settled in for what was to come.

"Good morning, Mr. President. Good morning, everyone. Ready to begin? Well, now," General Dimpey said, making deliberate eye contact with each of them. "Operation Persian Bomb has taken a few interesting turns. Last night the Pentagon received an emergency executive order to stand down in the Middle East. We received this order during the heat of combat, local Suez Canal time. It was a very difficult order to...implement. But I'm pleased to say that we've had enormous success in Operation Persian Bomb. Let me briefly recap the situation for you."

The wall viewscreens and computer screens changed to show a geographical map of Iran.

"Ten days ago," General Dimpey said, "the Iranians released three, twenty-megaton nuclear bombs from their bomb factory in Nantaz, in north-central Iran. The Israelis have been tracking the Iranian nuclear program and they have been providing us with valuable intel on the situation.

"One bomb was taken from Nantaz to the Persian Gulf by truck and loaded onto one of those VLCC hulks you saw a moment ago burning in the Suez Canal. Colonel Plummer got that nuke. I don't know how he managed to do it but he did. We had a missile cruiser in the Mediterranean on a fire mission for him, and we managed to sneak a SpecOps littoral submarine into the Persian Gulf to take away the nuke. However, the United States military command received emergency Presidential Executive Order 13666 that instructed the Unites States armed forces to immediately cease all military actions in the Persian Gulf. This included ongoing, hot combat operations. We obeyed the order."

General Dimpey looked sharply at the President.

"Colonel Plummer boarded the tankers and managed to get the bomb off before the order could be communicated to his SpecOps team. He succeeded in carrying out his mission, even without the Navy support we promised him."

The image on the main screens resolved into a map overview of the Persian Gulf. It zoomed in and changed to a live satellite view of the Persian Gulf entrance to the Suez Canal. The scene zoomed in closer and centered on a real time image of two VLCC oil tankers that had been run aground onto the shore of the Sinai Peninsula and blown up.

A haze of smoke covered the area. Huge boiling columns of black smoke climbed into the sky from each tanker. Large floating patches of oil burned in the water. The tankers had exploded and thrown out burning sheets of crude oil that blackened the light tan shoreline sands around the broken hulls. The water was covered in a burning, shimmering sheet of oil. A dozen Egyptian service boats and military vessels surrounded the blazing hulks. Ships passing through the edge of the vast oil slick left an iridescent wake that rippled in the sunlight. Egyptian helicopters flew over the tanker hulks and across the satellite image.

"This is where Colonel Plummer's Special Forces team air-assaulted the Iranian oil tankers," General Dimpey said. President Omeba sat up at the mention of Plummer's name. He remembered the insolent soldier he had ordered transferred to the Aleutian Islands. The last time he saw the man was just days ago, during his initial briefing on the Persian Bomb crisis. He looked sternly at Rahm and Valerie. Their tight, stiff expressions confirmed to him that they were looking at an extremely serious international incident.

"The Egyptians have closed the Suez Canal," General Dimpey continued. "It's been less than eighteen hours since Colonel Plummer's team hit the VLCCs, blew them up and left them burning on the shore. We think the Egyptians are going to keep the canal closed for a while to aggravate the situation and send us a message. They are *very* unhappy with us. We think they'll be even more unhappy with Iran when they learn that we retrieved a twenty kiloton nuclear weapon from an Iranian tanker in their canal."

He paused to allow the President's advisors a few moments to consider the situation. Omeba sat like a statue. Dimpey continued.

"The Iranians trucked a second bomb across Iran and Iraq, through Syria and into Lebanon, where it was staged at a Hamas camp in the Bekkah Valley. The Israelis fought their way into the terrorist camp and captured that nuke two hours after Plummer got our bomb. I don't know how they did it. We pulled the military support for that mission out from under the Israelis, too. We left them stranded in hostile enemy territory and under fire. But we obeyed Executive Order 13666. I sincerely hope it was worth it."

Rahm Adramelech interrupted General Dimpey.

"So you're saying to us that *despite* the Executive Order to the contrary, the United States military — *and* our Israeli allies — completed the missions we ordered stopped? Is that what you're telling us, General Dimpey?"

Dimpey looked at The Godfather with an unreadable expression.

"Um...sir...you must understand that the military operations were well under way when the President issued the order to recall them. It takes time to get an order of that magnitude down through all the right channels. Some of the operations couldn't be stopped. It was just too late. Ships and submarines were on station, with target coordinates ready to go. Helicopters with Special Forces units were en route to both the Suez Canal and to the Bekkah Valley. Stopping those military operations was a formidable task in itself. Despite all that, the mission was a success. We got the nuclear weapon we had targeted. Mission accomplished. You have to appreciate how capable our military forces really are, sir. They got the job done, even with less than a quarter of the assault and egress assets we planned to use. It's amazing really."

President Omeba drew in a long breath and held it. Those around the Situation Room conference table knew what was coming next. Whenever the President held his breath there was hell to pay. Omeba exhaled slowly, crossed his arms and shook his head.

"What's amazing to me," President Omeba said, "is how the United States Army and the Navy could continue missions that had already been cancelled by Executive Order. As your Commander in Chief, I want the names of everyone involved in this operation so that we can question them and understand exactly how all of this happened."

General Dimpey drew himself up. He knew the beginning of courts-martial when he saw it happening. He decided not to give the briefing he had planned to give.

"Mr. President...respectfully sir," he replied. "There is an eight-hour time difference between here and the Suez Canal. There was massive confusion over the orders," Dimpey said. "If you had explained the urgency of cancelling the mission, perhaps it would have been easier to get the missions stopped...in a more timely manner. You must understand, sir, that the Admirals and Generals in charge of this operation understood that they were intercepting Iranian nuclear bombs targeted for the United States or our allies. Many of our military commanders argued over the order. Some countermanded it. They didn't understand it. Frankly, respectfully sir, they didn't believe it could be happening. It took quite a bit of convincing — I can tell you — to get our military forces to withdraw after engagement with the enemy had commenced. And as for Colonel Plummer's Special Forces team, well they were engaged in the heat of combat and did not receive the order until after their mission action was completed. After that, well...operational security kept information transfers to an absolute minimum. The Joint Chiefs didn't see any reason to bother you until they had something new to report. And I am proud to report to you, Mr. President, that allied forces have captured two of the Iranian warheads. We have them in our possession."

President Omeba gave the military officer an incredulous face.

"Do you have a degree in law from Harvard, General Dimpey?" the President asked. The question dripped with contempt.

"No sir," General Dimpey said. "West Point: Class of 1964. Military command colleges after that. My master's degree is in engineering. MIT."

"And do you have an undergraduate degree from Colombia University?"

"No sir."

"There, you see?" President Omeba said. "All your education and experience is of a military nature. You have no grounding in law or international relations. You see things entirely from a military perspective."

"Yes sir. I do. This is a military operation."

"This is a United States government *kinetic action*, General Dimpey." President Omeba corrected. "We have a civilian government, do we not? Your Commander in Chief is a Harvard-educated law professor. Do you see my point, General?"

General Dimpey wavered. He understood the point perfectly, but knew it would be better not to say anything. The President's point was asinine. Vice President Bidet moved to speak but Rahm cut him off.

"We're getting off track here," Rahm said. He glowered at the military officer. "General, you understand that when you receive an Executive Order, that it is to be obeyed immediately, implicitly and to the best of your ability?"

"Yes sir."

"Then President Omeba's point is to be taken implicitly too. I want a list of names of those military officers that did not obey the President's Executive Order. I want this list delivered to me immediately. Is that clear?"

"Yes sir."

"And I want a written chronological summary of everything that happened between our last Operation Persian Bomb briefing and this one. Got that?"

"Yes sir."

"Good. Then get on with your briefing, General," Rahm instructed. "We have more important things to get to today."

"Yes sir. Ah...well...the two thermonuclear bombs. They have been secured and are no longer a threat to the United States or to Israel."

Janet Napolitburo had been brooding on something she'd heard earlier. She made a face and said, "Where is Colonel Plummer's team now? And where is the bomb he took off the

Iranian tanker? I understand the Israelis have the bomb from the Hamas camp in the Bekkah Valley. Is that right? Where is the other one? Isn't there another one? I'm missing a bomb somehow."

"Colonel Plummer *did* retrieve the bomb from the VLCC," General Dimpey said carefully. "He removed it using one of his Chinooks. He transferred the bomb to the Israelis for safekeeping."

A chorus of hisses sounded around the table. Omeba's hand slapped the table top in disgust. Someone muttered that the Muslims were not our enemies. But Janet Napolitburo raised her finger to keep her line of questioning going through the hubub. She was interested in the bomb she understood was destined for New York City.

"So *our* bomb isn't coming to the United States? I want to confirm that," Janet Napolitburo said. "At least we at Homeland Defense don't have to worry about *that* one."

"What about the third bomb?" Vice President Bidet asked, picking up on Napolitburo's line of thought. "That's what Janet is asking you about. You said there were three nukes. Where's the third bomb?"

Everyone looked at General Dimpey.

"The Israelis have both of the bombs that were retrieved from the Persian Gulf," Dimpey replied. "We don't know where the third bomb is. We never had any track on it at all. No intelligence information whatsoever. We simply don't know. And now that the Israelis have stopped sharing their intelligence with us, we're completely in the dark."

President Omeba swore.

"You talk to the Israelis way too much, General Dimpey," Omeba said. "And now you're telling me that there's one more Persian Bomb out there that could still be coming our way? Do you realize how badly the military has screwed up this situation? I had already produced a diplomatic solution to the crisis. That's why I gave you the order to stand down military operations. You didn't. And now we have a major international incident on our hands!"

The President was incredulous. The military had taken a bad situation and made it unfathomably worse. What would he say to Mahmoud now? And after all of the military bungling and screw-ups there was still more bad news. There was another bomb out there somewhere. After what the military had done to the Iranian tankers, he couldn't expect any more help from Mahmoud.

Rahm bent over and whispered into the President's ear. The President's eyes widened; then he nodded.

"Right," President Omeba said. "General Dimpey, you will personally order all American and allied military forces in the Middle Eastern theater restricted to their bases. Immediately. You will recall all of the Special Forces teams — *all* of them. Get them out of the Middle East. I want the Admiral Stennis carrier and its battle group pulled out of the Persian Gulf and sent as far away from Arab territory as you can get them. I want full implementation of Executive Order 13666."

"What? Sir?" General Dimpey couldn't believe his ears. The Situation Room buzzed with exclamations of astonishment.

"You heard me, General," President Omeba barked. "And I want *all* of you military-types in this room to understand me as well. You leave the Middle East alone. That's an order. You have to stop persecuting the Muslims. You people do not have law degrees from Harvard. You do not understand these things. I order you to cancel Operation Persian Bomb in its entirety."

Gasps of disappointment and disbelief filled the Situation Room. This only angered Omeba further.

"I'll call President Ahmanutjob personally," he said coldly. "Mahmoud and I understand one another. I'll see if I can salvage our relationship after this fiasco you military people have created. Rahm and Leon will follow up to make sure that you all do what you've been ordered to do. You are all dismissed!"

The President gave them all a steely look to make sure they understood how serious he was about these orders. Then he collected his papers and left the Situation Room. The National Security Team trailed behind.

General Dimpey glared after them. His chief aide, a two-star general came up to him.

"General Dimpey, this is serious," he said. "We can't just let that third bomb roam loose like this. I feel sure it'll make its way here. It would be a national catastrophe if it detonated in New York...or here in Washington, D.C. We have to stop it."

"You heard the President," General Dimpey said, still staring at the door the President and his entourage had just passed through. "Operation Persian Bomb has been officially terminated. We have been ordered by the Commander in Chief to stand down."

"But we can't *do* that," the two-star protested. "We can't just sit on our thumbs and let millions of innocent Americans get killed."

General Dimpey looked at his distressed friend and comrade.

"Do you remember your service oath?" he asked.

"I sure do."

"Then remember it now," General Dimpey said. "We swore to defend the United States Constitution against all enemies...foreign *and* domestic. And we swore to obey the Commander in Chief and all officers appointed over us."

"Yes. I remember."

"Then that's what we'll do," Dimpey said. "We will officially stand down Operation Persian Bomb. But there's something I didn't mention in the briefing: Colonel Plummer is still out there.

He's actively looking for that missing bomb. He needs our help. If we can't help him *officially*, then perhaps we can help him unofficially."

"But how? We can't use the CIA. Leon Panera *owns* the CIA. Last month he was the Director of the CIA."

"We can do it. I'll do it. We still have friends and allies, in the CIA and elsewhere. It'll mean my career, but there's one thing a helluva lot more important than our careers."

"What's that, sir?"

"There's a nuclear bomb loose out there somewhere. It's got our name on it. I can feel it. We've got to find it before it finds us."

11

REPORTING FROM THE BBC

G avin Bond stood patiently in front of the White House as the makeup girl pancaked the last touches of powder onto his cheeks. Gavin was the most renowned journalist and news presenter in the British Broadcasting Corporation. He specialized in American presidential politics and had won a bevy of prestigious awards for his coverage of Jimmuh Carper, Ronald Regal, Bill Clitman, George Boosh, and now — Barak Omeba.

Bond believed that he was working the most important story of his career: the downfall of the United States of America. Gavin wanted to be the journalist of record for this historic transition. The BBC correspondent believed he had a special obligation to truthfully record his observations and report them to the world. But he knew it would be difficult for him to maintain professional objectivity and journalistic detachment, as this was a personal matter for him. Unlike most foreign journalists, Gavin loved America and the Americans. His idea of heaven was a cabin near a trout stream in the Colorado mountains, where there were no telephones and no email. He loved cheeseburgers, cowboys, the friendliness of the people, football and the free and open liberty of the country. His dream was to own a Winnebago and travel the byways throughout the length and breadth of America. It broke his heart to see what was happening to this great nation.

And he had a hard time believing that the rest of the world stood idly by watching, offering no help whatsoever — even snickering as America's suicidal self-destruction slowly unfolded. The irony was that the same socialist-induced, multicultural self-destruction was happening to all of the other western nations as well. But the imminent fall of the once invincible United States was by far the most consequential. The last great hope of mankind was dying a ludicrous death, the victim of everything it had once stood against.

Gavin likened the fate of America to that of the maiden voyage of the mighty Titanic steamship. The Captain and crew of the great vessel knew of the extreme danger of icebergs in those dangerous waters — much like the leadership of the United States knew full well the perils of flirting with socialism. But they ignored the imminent danger, sailed directly into the fatal hazard, and now found themselves gutted and sinking in cold indifferent waters.

Gavin imagined what it must be like to be an American, like a Titanic survivor shivering in a pitching lifeboat, watching the majestic ship of state slip by inches down into its cold, watery grave. Gavin felt helpless being unable to do anything about it. It was like being at the deathbed of a loved one. There was little you could do except comfort them and say goodbye.

The least he could do was record the final passing of the land and people he loved. Gavin Bond alone had the power and influence in the BBC to demand six months on assignment in America, to cover the debacle of the Omeba Administration and America's degradation and descent into third world nation status.

The makeup lady stepped back for a final inspection. She nodded to him. He raised his microphone and smiled. The cameraman was ready. Gavin composed himself and began.

"Gavin Bond here, reporting for the BBC. As I travel about the United States, I feel like I'm in a police state. At every train station and airport, there are government police watching you, demanding your papers, searching your luggage — even putting their hands in your knickers and feeling your privates for a bomb or box cutter. Surveillance cameras are everywhere. You cannot go into a government building without passing through security screening and a metal detector. The United States of America is no longer the Land of Liberty: it is the Land of the Lost, or as Lush Rimshot calls it: 'Zombieland'. Is the Omeba administration deliberately bringing about the demise of the once greatest nation on earth? Many Americans think so, and we are here in America to discover the truth behind this historic tragedy."

The camera panned over Gavin's shoulder and zoomed into the north portico of the White House, with its beautiful white columns. Pennsylvania Avenue was a favorite place for reporters to stand and opine on matters of great consequence. The White House made a wonderful backdrop for news reporting. Gavin had broadcast from here many times over the last thirty years. It was fitting that he begin the series on *The Decline and Fall of America* from this vantage point.

"The American Dream has become a nightmare for many in America," Gavin said. "The unemployment rate stands at eighteen point six percent. The government tells the people that it is at nine percent, but no one believes them anymore. Americans can't find jobs to pay their way. A quarter of the citizens are in the process of losing their homes. The national debt has officially topped twenty trillion dollars; an amount that most observers agree cannot *ever* be paid off. And the actual amount is believed to be much higher than what the government says it is. Informed sources place the actual American debt at over fifty trillion dollars. The government says the economy is improving but nobody believes it. And that is one of the major problems for Americans in these difficult days.

"America has become a nation that cannot believe *anything* that their government tells them. They cannot believe what their news media or political leadership tells them. Much of what Americans see, hear and read in the establishment media simply isn't true. Americans have been lied to by so many, for so long, that they are a nation that cannot depend on any traditional source of information to hear the truth. Americans live in a Culture of Deception.

"The fact is that Americans do not know what the truth is anymore. And a people who lack the truth cannot deal with reality; they cannot make informed rational decisions to solve their problems. Without the truth, people cannot find their way. A nation without truth is a land of the lost. Americans are truly lost in Zombieland."

Gavin nodded at the cameraman and twirled his finger over his head, indicating a wrap.

"That should do for our opening segment," Bond said. "I think it went very well."

The makeup girl nodded vigorously in agreement. The cameraman said, "Perfect, Boss. Let's call it a day."

Gavin nodded his approval. Just then his cell phone binged, indicating the arrival of an email. He checked his iPhone and found it was a message he would want to read immediately. The email was encrypted and had a red flag priority. It was important. It was from the BBC office in Cairo.

***

The British Broadcasting Corporation had excellent contacts and sources in the Middle East. Gavin Bond couldn't believe what he was reading in the encrypted email that was just sent to him by the Middle East Bureau Chief. If it was true, it was the news story of the year. As far as he knew, none of the American news media had an inkling of what was going on. They certainly weren't reporting anything.

As a high-profile BBC television newsreader, Gavin had the clout and the contacts to get to the bottom of any story. He called top-level contacts at ABC, NPR, CBS, MSNBC, and CNN. His name was enough to get him straight through on each call. He had a long, evasive conversation with the news director at NPR, who figured out he was on to something big. But he was careful in his questioning and gave little away. He had the makings of a spectacular news scoop and he wasn't about to alert a competitor.

Gavin figured that a trip to the Suez Canal was impossible for him, but he could send an assistant. He called the Middle East Bureau Chief on his iPhone.

"Trevor," Gavin said. "Hello. How's the Sphinx?"

"Hello to you, Gavin," Trevor Howard replied jovially, "The Sphinx is bloody awful. I see you've received my email."

"That's why I'm calling. Did you perchance tell anyone else about the goings on in the Suez Canal?"

"Not yet," Trevor replied. "I wanted you to have first go at it."

"I appreciate that," Gavin said.

"I want a favor in return."

"Of course."

"There's more news," Trevor said. "The Suez Canal has been officially closed. I'm at the Cairo office and I can tell you the city is in a state of absolute bedlam. The Egyptian military is going dotty as well. They're scrambling jets and getting half their army rolling to the eastern end of the canal. There are several tankers afire inside the canal and I have reports of black helicopters engaging the Egyptian army. Our contacts swear that the Jews are attacking, but I think it might be the Americans. Something big is going on and I'm sure the Yanks are in the middle of it. You better get here quick."

Gavin Bond pondered the bombshell information. It could be the beginning of a new Middle East war...possibly World War III. He felt in his bones that this was going to be a blockbuster story. But he was onto something even more important.

"I can't come to Egypt," Gavin said. "I'm onto something bigger. But I can dispatch a team."

"Bigger? What could be bigger?"

"It's much bigger, Trevor my friend. It's the biggest story in the history of modern civilization: the decline and fall of the United States of America, and I'm standing right in the middle of it."

12

CABINET MEETING

Valerie Garrotte walked rapidly through the West Wing corridor to the Cabinet Room. She looked into the Lewdinsky Room next to the Oval Office to see if Barry was there. He was not. A sudden memory of being alone in that room with Barry consumed her for a moment. When she came out of it she realized she had lost her original train of thought. She stood there and tried to remember what was so urgent that she had to find Barry and talk to him about it. She knew it was something she had to pretend was true. But she could not remember what it was she was supposed to be pretending this time. It was getting confusing.

Everyone in the White House pretended that things were a certain way, because those things were the official position of the administration. All administrations did that to some degree. But the people in President Omeba's bubble had to remember countless items that were not true, but had to be acted on as if they were — even in the face of the most dire and blatant contradiction.

Liberals, however, possessed the intellectual faculty of cognitive dissonance — the ability to simultaneously hold contradictory beliefs, without having their thinking processes break down. Normal people could not do this.

But even Rahm had to maintain a spreadsheet to keep things straight and ensure that party members stayed consistent with administration policy. The news media covered for the administration, of course. But they couldn't cloak *all* of Barak Omeba's magical thinking, especially when it came to foreign policy or the economy. Blowback from those politically charged arenas was often too severe to deny or gloss over.

Things had drifted so far away from reality that even *she* was having trouble keeping up with the illusions, embellishments, spin, prevarication, invention, subterfuge, inaccuracies, deceit, distractions, evasions, falsehoods and forgeries being fostered by the White House. Matters were getting out of hand.

The Cabinet Room was packed with people. Once Valerie arrived, Rahm rapped his water glass with his spoon and called the meeting to order.

"Alright everyone, we've got a full agenda today so get your notebooks. Let's get to work."

Rahm looked at the faces around the table and at the people in chairs lined against the wall, to see that everybody was doing what he told them to do. He wasn't called The Godfather for nothing. You did what Rahm told you to do, or you paid dearly for it. No exceptions. Even the President was afraid of him.

"There are three agenda items today," Rahm announced. "As usual, we'll take the agenda items in reverse order so that we end up focused on our top priority. Our third priority item is jobs."

"Shouldn't that be our *number one* priority?" Vice President Bidet asked. "Look...the number-one priority facing the middle class is a three-letter word: jobs. J-O-B-S, jobs."

Rahm rolled his eyes. He chose to ignore the Vice President. He looked over to the President with an arched eyebrow. President Omeba took his cue. Rahm said the President had to show more leadership in Cabinet meetings. No more leading from behind. But Omeba knew that Rahm was really running the meeting. So did everyone else.

"We need to get the unemployment numbers down," the President said, looking to Rahm and Valerie for approval. "We're showing a 9.9% unemployment rate again this month. That's up from the 9.1% number we've been releasing for the last two years."

"It's really closer to 18.6%, sir," Timothy Geitmare said.

"You shut the hell up!" Rahm spat, looking irritably around the table. Rahm scowled at everyone to make damn sure they got the message. The real unemployment number was *never* to be spoken aloud.

"It *has* to be less than 10%. It can *never* be more than 10% — no matter *what* happens. That's the magic number." Rahm scowled at the Treasury Secretary; then looked at the President, who spoke.

"We need to get the numbers down so we can show the people we're making progress on the jobs front," Omeba said, reading from his teleprompter notes. "If we don't get the unemployment numbers down, then our chances for reelection are not good."

The room was quiet for a moment. Not a single Cabinet Member uttered a sound. None of them had a clue about how to create jobs. Not one of them had ever worked in the private sector.

"Well, sir. People just aren't hiring," Hilda Hoffa said. She was Secretary of the Department of Labor. "They don't have any faith in the economy. That's the problem with capitalism. You can't just make companies hire workers in this country. It's not at all like creating government jobs in Europe or someplace civilized."

"Just get the numbers down," Omeba ordered. "It doesn't matter how you do it."

"Well, sir..." Hilda offered. "We've stopped counting people working part time, and we've stopped counting new graduates and people coming out of the military. We now assume they aren't even looking for work, since there's none to be found. That brought the numbers down quite a bit after the last time we had this meeting. No one even squawked about that."

"You need to do more," Rahm countered. "We need to find more people not to count. How about not counting people who haven't worked in over a year? They've stopped working — haven't they? I bet most of them have decided to retire or live on welfare."

"Maybe if we looked at not counting people who have run out of unemployment benefits," Valerie Garrotte offered. "We've extended unemployment benefits to forty months — that's over three years. If they haven't found a job in three years they're not going to."

"How about the people on welfare?" Kathleen Cerberus asked. She was the Secretary of Health and Human Services. "They're not working and don't have to. Most of them have never worked. We might as well not count them as unemployed. I don't see why we can't just deduct them from the unemployment totals."

"That's it!" the President declared. "I think you people are onto something here. After three years of unemployment benefits those people have forgotten how to work. So don't count them any more. And Kathleen's idea is good too. Don't count the people on welfare either. We've got the welfare rolls up to a record high. Hilda — how much can you get the numbers down if you stop counting all those people?"

The Labor Secretary consulted an aide who had a laptop running the figures. Hilda Hoffa looked at the results and did a double take.

"9.6%! You're a *genius*, Mr. President," she declared.

Omeba demurred, smiling immodestly.

"There's always more than one way to skin a raccoon. Progressive thinking opens up creative pathways for solving problems. Too bad we can't get the Republicans to think the way we do."

"Most of them are coming around, Barry," Vice President Bidet said. He'd served seven terms in the Senate and knew the opposition quite well. He was drinking buddies with the establishment Republicans. "More than half of the Republicans are establishment RINOS these days. Even some of the new ones are big government Republicans. They pretty much think the way we do."

The President gave a slight nod in partial agreement. "Yes. Well, maybe some of them see the light: Grayham and McStain, for example. But most of the new Tea Party congressmen want to return to Constitutional government. We've got to cure them of that."

Rahm checked his watch and drummed the table. The room went instantly quiet.

"That gets us to our number two priority," Rahm said. "It's pretty obvious since the mid-term election that we're not going to get anything else through Congress. We did pretty well in the three years when we had both houses of Congress. But the midterms wiped out our majority in the House and decreased it in the Senate.

"Yeah," Joe Bidet agreed. "We rammed some frickin' big stuff through when we had both houses."

Rahm gave a rare nod of approval to the Vice President.

"That's true, Joe. We've implemented a large part of our agenda already. In fact, our accomplishments have been nothing short of incredible. In our first year, we took over the health care industry with OmebaCare. That was one fifth of the American economy in one fell swoop, despite the fact that the vast majority of the American people were adamantly opposed to the legislation. But that one piece of legislation is the hook we vitally needed to ensure progressive socialist government in the United States. It's just a matter of time now.

"We paid back our political supporters with Stimulus I and II. We took over the banking and insurance industries with TARP. We took the auto industry away from the capitalists and gave it to the United Auto Workers union. Our party took over the housing industry by creating the subprime mortgage crisis, and then bailing out Fannie Mae and Freddy Mac. FHA is next, thanks to Barney Fag. We took over Wall Street and the banking industries with the Dodd-Frank Act.

"We've swung our borders wide open to immigrants and sued states who have tried to stop the undocumented new voters from coming in. We passed the Hate Crimes Prevention Act so that people who disagree with sexual freedom for deviants are punished for openly expressing their opinions. We have materially expanded homosexual education and indoctrination in elementary and middle schools across the nation."

"We fired two wartime Generals right off the battlefield for disagreeing with our conduct of the Afghanistan and Iraq wars. We abolished *Don't Ask, Don't Tell* so that our soldiers can openly commit sodomy in uniform. We achieved parity with Russia by reducing our nuclear arms capabilities and giving them our most advanced top-secret military technologies. We ensured that the Chinese military was able to expand and improve its technological reach by sharing our missile technology with them. We transferred our economy to theirs so that they could build up their military. The Chinese blue water navy will be able to control the Sea of Japan in just a few years. They will have space-based weapons platforms decades before anyone else, including us."

Rahm's voice rose as he continued to recite their achievements. The excitement in the Cabinet Room increased with each victory.

"Our Environmental Protection Agency has been instrumental in curbing a runaway economy. The EPA has helped us attack the use of coal in the production of electricity and the use of petroleum for anything. We now have green solutions to produce electricity and create government jobs. We've shut down petroleum drilling in the Gulf of Mexico, Alaska and off the Atlantic and Pacific coasts. We stopped the XL pipeline from Canada. We've stopped all inland exploration, mining and drilling. We're on the way to shutting down shale oil too.

"People, we've transferred a fantastic amount of wealth and accomplished a tremendous amount of work in our first three years," Rahm exclaimed to cheers and applause. "We should be proud of our legislative accomplishments!"

Rahm Adramelech pounded the table with the flat of his hand for emphasis. The room burst into loud and raucous cheers and whistles. People pounded the table, stamped their feet and hooted. Hillary sang *The Marseillaise*, but nobody else knew the words. These were the true believers, the fellow travelers extraordinaire. These were the progressives that Omeba had found to run the government and change it forever. Eric Holdup and Janet Napolitburo held each other and cried tears of joy. Rahm was right! They had accomplished a great deal in the time they had so far. Each of them had plunged diligently into their jobs, boring deep into the walls and foundations of the American house like a billion hungry termites. They had succeeded enormously in undermining the very foundations of American culture, society, government and the economy.

"But now we've got a big problem," Rahm continued, looking sternly at everyone. It was time to mute the festivity and return to progressive reality. "Now the Repugs control the House and they have a strong minority in the Senate. We can't get any legislation passed and we can't increase spending. That's our main problem. We have to increase spending to secure our voter base. Red Harry won't produce a budget in the Senate, even if he is required by the Constitution to do so. He knows the Repugs won't officially approve the trillion and a half dollar increase we put in the budget. So we're stymied. We can no longer cram our agenda through the Senate, and we've lost the House, for now. We can't get any new legislation passed."

"I witness that thought," Vice President Bidet agreed. "That's a problem. So what can we do about it?"

Rahm looked to President Omeba, who took his cue.

"We go *around* Congress," the President said. "Since Mohammed won't go to the mountain...the mountain must come to Mohammed."

Perplexed looks passed among those around the table.

"If Congress won't pass the laws that we want, then we'll just use executive orders and the regulatory agencies to get things done," Omeba explained. "It's simple."

Several Cabinet Members looked uncertain. Something seemed wrong with this plan. This was outside the normal legislative process. In fact, this was completely outside any *legislative* process.

"I see Constitutional issues here," Eric Holdup said. "People are going to question whether or not what we're doing is Constitutional."

The others laughed.

"Are you *serious*?" Rahm asked. "The Constitution is not a factor any more. We'll just go around it like we have been. Like we're getting ready to go around Congress. We have a revolutionary agenda that takes priority. We work from that. Listen carefully. We *own* the rules and regulations production complex. The bureaucrats who run it work for us. They answer to us — the Executive Branch of government. And if Congress won't get the job done, then we'll just bypass those dinosaurs and do it ourselves."

"That's right," Omeba affirmed. "We can't wait! We can't expect our political enemies or the American people to agree with every little thing we want to do. So we've got to be the adults in the room and take charge of things ourselves. We'll use the regulatory bureaucracy to get everything done. And I'll issue the executive orders. To hell with Congress. We can't wait."

A rumble of conversation ensued as the Cabinet Members considered what this would mean to them personally. Some of them liked the idea. But this new approach to running over one hundred and thirty executive departments meant they had a lot of work to do. If they could now bypass Congress and the legislative process, then they could also bypass federal legislative and procurement regulations and guidelines. They could ignore public comment and political opposition. They could ignore cost/benefit analysis and public disclosure rules. They could ignore the Paperwork Reduction Act. It was a giddy prospect. But they needed some guidance on how to proceed. Rahm was way ahead of them. He turned to the EPA Administrator, Lisa Jackoff.

"Folks, Lisa here is a wonderful example of what we can do with our regulatory agencies. She has done a bang-up job using the regulatory process to get our agenda moving forward. She got carbon dioxide declared hazardous to human health and the environment, even though carbon dioxide is essential to life on Earth, and everyone on the planet is breathing it right this moment. She single-handedly reinterpreted the Clean Air Act to implement greenhouse gas emission standards for automobiles. Now she's going after coal-fired power plants under the MACT rules. We'll have Cap and Trade and Carbon Taxes pretty soon — in spite of the Repugs and Tea Baggers in Congress. She's working with the United Nations and the IPCC to make the global warming framework work for us. That will open up an entirely new arena of taxation, wealth transfer and global government. Good work, Lisa. Now that's what I call creative destruction. People, if you have any questions about using your agency to pass new rules and regulations to do things Congress will not, you just have to ask Lisa for guidance. She's a genius at getting around the legislative process. Bravo, Lisa."

Everyone applauded the EPA Administrator. She *really* knew how to operate a bureaucracy and get the most out of it.

"You can do similar things in your agencies and departments," Rahm continued. "You will each draw up a list of progressive regulations that you want to push through your agencies and departments. We'll chart a path for you to force them through the regulatory system and into the Code of Federal Regulations. We own the Government Printing Office. We can print our own rules and regulations. This way we can bypass both the Congress and the Constitution in one fell swoop. That's Item Two on the agenda, and I think we've got a good start on it," Rahm said. "Now let's get down to our top priority."

"You mean the Iranian nuclear bombs being transported secretly into the country?" Vice President Bidet asked aloud.

Rahm Adramelech scowled angrily at the Vice President. "That's top secret, *you idiot*," he hissed. "Now the entire Cabinet and all of their aides know about it."

Joe Bidet looked around the long table at a sea of frightened faces. Yes. They did hear him. No doubt about it.

"I was just joking," Bidet offered, smiling idiotically, waving his hands as if to swish the words away. "There really aren't any nuclear weapons loose out there...heading our way. Not really. The CIA and military aren't looking for them."

Rahm palmed his face.

"Our *number one* priority, people," the Chief of Staff said, looking hatefully at the Vice President, "is the re-election campaign. We've got a few new wrinkles. They're serious and we have to deal with them. Our most serious of these problems is the matter of public dissent. There's too much of it. And there's a group of people out there running around calling themselves The Patriots who are causing all kinds of problems."

"The Patriots?" Lisa Jackoff asked. "What's that?"

"Trouble," President Omeba said. "The most serious kind of trouble we could possibly be facing. We have a grass-roots uprising on our hands."

13

BRAINSTREAM MEDIA

After the Cabinet Meeting, Rahm gathered the Inner Circle in the Situation Room for a crisis management meeting. Three days after the blowup with General Dimpey in that same room, the Persian Bomb crisis was old news. Rahm had a much bigger problem that had to be dealt with. The American people were becoming intractable — even belligerent — and the election was only months away. Something had to be done about them. Present were President Omeba, Eric Holdup, Gay Corney, Leon Panera, Janet Napolitburo, Joe Bidet and Valerie Garrotte.

Eric Holdup stepped outside the Situation Room. He reappeared a few moments later with a middle-aged man wearing a crumpled pinstriped blue suit. He had a head of thin greasy black hair and watery blue eyes. Something about his eyes looked familiar. He was a fellow traveler, no doubt about it. He had the look. Probably a friend of Dorothy's too. He looked like an ACLU lawyer but he wasn't. He was a behavioral technology scientist — a psychoengineer — and an internet entrepreneur. He strode over to President Omeba and took his hand.

"It is an honor, sir, to meet you at last," the man said sincerely. His accent was thick, perhaps East German. He sounded very much like Henry Kissinger.

"This is Doctor Winfrey Soros, Mr. President," Eric Holdup introduced. "He's a friend of ours. He's the brains behind Act Up, MoveOn.org, Democrats Underground and a dozen other progressive political and fund raising organizations. He's the one who came up with the *Yes We Can* and *Hope and Change* campaign slogans. Dr. Soros is a trailblazer into the brave new world we're working to bring about."

A murmur of oohs and aahs swept the room. President Omeba was astonished. This was the reclusive Dr. Winfrey Soros of progressive fame and legend. Omeba instantly respected the man. They all did. Some revered him.

Dr. Soros was a delicate man, weak looking. He had pale skin and large puffy eyes, his face was pocked with ancient acne scars, which spoke of a lonely adolescence. His greasy black hair was combed straight back. He looked ill. But to the true believers in the room, he was perceived as a giant of a man, a genius: the greatest political technowizard of all time. He used his specialized knowledge to amass a fortune via the internet and mass media. He was a billionaire.

When Barak Hussein Omeba entered politics, Winfrey Soros knew where he was going to put his money and talent. Money and media was what the politician needed, and Soros had both in abundance. Soros not only donated and raised hundreds of millions of dollars for candidate Omeba, he also gave him the electronic media power punch that catapulted him into the White House.

"Dr. Soros is somewhat of a celebrity in his rarified field," Holdup said. "He's a wizard in the business of using mass media technology to influence human behavior. He pioneered the field of psychoengineering and founded the internet colossus Moogle. He's firmly in our camp, Mr. President. I personally vouch for him. He's here today to talk to you about some research he's been conducting for the re-election campaign. What he's discovered is mind-blowing, to say the least. You need to listen to him. Our entire agenda could depend on it."

President Omeba was suitably impressed. He'd known Eric for over twenty years and he'd never given such a glowing recommendation for anyone.

"Okay, Dr. Soros," the President said. "I'm listening."

Soros sat for a moment with his head down and hands folded, like he was in prayer. Then he looked up sharply at the President.

"You are a *liar*, Mr. President," he said forcefully and with certainty. "At no time are you ever telling the truth about anything."

Shocked gasps filled the room. President Omeba looked at Dr. Soros, unfazed.

"So?" Omeba replied. He had been called a liar many times in his life. Someone was always calling him a liar about something. He thought of lying as an art form, and nothing to be ashamed of. It was a talent he had perfected during a lifetime of deception. Omeba felt he was a much better liar than Bill Clitman. Deception was the source of his power. To him, being called a liar was a compliment.

"The problem, Mr. President," Dr. Soros continued, "is that people are beginning to catch on. They're seeing *through* you now. Your shtick just isn't working anymore, at least not for many people. They see you as a bullshit artist."

"Now that *is* bullshit," Omeba said confidently. "The American people will buy anything I say."

"The public perception used to be that you were telling the truth, that you were sincere," Soros continued, unruffled. "After all, nobody would even *think* that a Presidential candidate, and especially an elected President, could ever lie as much as you do. But you lie all the time. You lie constantly. At no time are you not lying. And that has caused a dangerous public perception problem that we have to deal with. The majority of the public doesn't believe *most* of what you say. Not any more. About a third of the people don't believe anything you say. Even your core thirty-five percent of government employees, union members and welfare recipients don't believe you. But they don't count. They don't care whether you're lying to them or not. They get the bread and circuses anyway. It's the rest of the public that we have to be concerned about."

Omeba looked at Dr. Soros with pained disbelieving eyes.

"Is it really that bad?" Omeba asked, "Really? Rahm do *you* think so too? Valerie?"

His two closest advisors nodded their heads.

"I have been feeling a bit stale lately..."

Dr. Soros regarded the President oddly for a few moments; then began again.

"Do you even *know* about the zombies, Mr. President?"

"What the hell is that all about anyway?" Omeba demanded. "That's all my press secretary wants to talk about. The media buzz is all about the *zombies*: people wandering around mindlessly in the streets; people zoned out in their businesses and workplaces. What's up with that?"

"Gay Corney should know," Soros said. "Let's look at the current situation in another way. For example, one of the great mysteries of the political world is how you won the election against the Republican establishment Senator Juan McStain."

"I smoked that old fart."

"Yes, you did," Dr. Soros agreed. "You managed to get a great number of people to believe that you were *The One* they had been waiting for. They didn't even know they were waiting for anybody. But you sold them on the idea. You could make a fortune in advertising, Mr. President."

"Well...I can't take all the credit," Omeba replied. "Nancy, Harry and the media spent the previous eight years tearing down the Boosh presidency. By the time they were done sabotaging the government, everyone in America wanted to throw Boosh and the Republicans out of office. That worked in our favor too."

"The news media were *central* to the success of your election," Soros agreed. "They reinforced the idea in the minds of the voters that America needed hope and change — especially *change*. The media programmed the people to want *change* more than anything. We had this message circulating in an endless loop through the media. The media funneled the votes to you. Millions of Americans flocked to your bandwagon. They were drawn like iron filings to a magnet, like moths to a flame. They believed in you. They believed in the change you offered them. You gave them hope. They expected miraculous things from you because of the incessant media messages they brainstreamed through their television sets.

"The Republicans stood around flat-footed, astonished at what was happening to them. They watched helplessly as you sucked the oxygen from the political atmosphere. There was nothing they could do. The media carried your water and made it happen," Dr. Soros said. "But it was *our* team that produced the carefully worded subliminal messages that brainstreamed the groupmind of the masses. We fed the subliminal messages to the internet sites, the DNC, and to the media. It was *my* group that wrote your speeches and subliminally inserted your message of hope and change into the minds of the zombies for you."

"We brainstreamed them into the groupmind through the television sets. We delivered our psychoengineered programming through the human visual cortex. Human beings believe what they see. Seeing is believing, as they say. Vision accounts for more than ninety-nine percent of our informational input. Information our brains receive through the visual cortex is always regarded as true. This is why television is so effective in the indoctrination of the groupmind. This is how we brainstream people into becoming progressive zombies."

President Omeba turned to his most trusted friend and advisor — Valerie Garrotte. She nodded back at him.

"It's true, Barry," she said. "Dr. Soros wrote all of your material. He's the one who wrote your most famous speeches. And it was he who insisted that you not be left alone in front of a camera or microphone. It was Dr. Soros who insisted that you use a teleprompter. But it was you, Barry, who delivered the message and brought the voters stampeding in to support you."

Barak stared at Valerie, then at Rahm and the others. He was astonished at what he'd just learned. They all nodded in the affirmative. They were all in on it. He thought Valerie and Rahm had written all of his speeches and insisted on the changes in his presentation style. Now he knew that they had hired an expert to manipulate public opinion to help the cause. It worked brilliantly. Dr. Soros had obviously contributed greatly to his success.

And now his Inner Circle had brought the man back, evidently to work more magic on the re-election campaign. This was a good thing. Omeba smiled at them.

"Yeah. The campaign was a lot of hard work," the President said. "But we sold the dream."

"You are the wizard that made it happen," Soros replied.

"I am the Lightworker," Omeba countered, warming to Dr. Soros.

"You are the magician."

"I am The One."

"You are the conduit."

"I am the Messiah."

"You are the sorcerer who made the zombies."

"I am...wha...the what?"

"You do know what a zombie is, don't you, Mr. President?"

"Yes. Sure. Zombies come from East African voodoo. A zombie is someone who comes back from the dead and feeds on the living." President Omeba was perplexed by this sudden change in the direction of the conversation.

"Not a bad description, but there's more," Dr. Soros said. "A zombie has no will of its own. The creature is made by magical means or witchcraft: by a wizard or sorcerer. It is an animated corpse, largely unaffected by reality — by what is actually going on around it. It has no self-awareness, no ability to think for itself. It just stumbles along, feeding on others. The zombie is totally subject to the will of the sorcerer who created it. The zombie does whatever the sorcerer tells it to do. It doesn't even think about the commands it is given. It just obeys them — whatever they are. Whatever the sorcerer tells it to do."

"Wow."

"Yes, Mr. President, exactly. Wow. Zombies. Today we call them *progressives*. Or you may prefer to call them liberals, Democrats or socialists. There is no difference."

"Are you calling my supporters and followers *zombies*?"

"Yes. That's it. Exactly," Dr. Soros said. "Democratic Party voters are zombies. They are completely unable to think for themselves. They depend on the media, the government — and you in particular — to do their thinking for them.

"They cheer when I blow my nose."

"That's them! Isn't that amazing, Mr. President? It's astonishing, in fact. But the problem is that only about a third of the people are totally zombie."

"We're working on that."

"I know. I'm on the team doing the work. But we've got serious problems. No patriotic American would ever vote for you. Not now. They've had four years to see what you're really up to. And that makes your zombies more important to us than ever. Your hardcore zombies make up thirty-five percent of the vote — a very reliable socialist voting bloc. You'll have them forever — at least as long as their government checks keep coming. But a large number of zombies are beginning to wake up," Dr. Soros explained. "We call them Undecided Zombies. The Undecided Zombies constitute about twenty percent of the vote. *They're* the problem. We're losing this twenty percent very rapidly. And we can't get re-elected with only thirty five percent of the vote. There are powerful forces working to break the spell...er...the enthralling regard the masses have for you."

"The Tea Party? Sure, they're a problem. You can't be talking about the Republicans. The Patriots? Maybe. They're new. Lush Rimshot!" the President exclaimed. "That guy has been plaguing me since before the *first* election campaign. Do you know he called me a Magic Negro and got away with it?"

"Yessir," Soros agreed. "Lush Rimshot is indeed causing you a lot of serious damage. No doubt about it. His most damaging effect is rallying the opposition base against you. He reinforces all the patriotic and Constitutional nonsense we've been trying to get rid of for the past fifty years."

"He's ruining me."

"Yessir. Lush Rimshot is a menace to the progressive cause. But he isn't what I'm talking about. He's the tip of the iceberg. He's like Paul Revere. But he's not the real problem."

"You mean there's more?" the President demanded, horrified at the thought of something even worse for him than Lush Rimshot and his AM radio show. What could be worse than Lush Rimshot?

Dr. Soros leaned forward. The others in the room leaned forward as well, not wanting to miss anything uttered by this astonishing man.

"What can we do, Dr. Soros?" the Vice President asked.

The billionaire internet mogul made a tent of his hands. He leaned further forward. Omeba leaned forward to meet him. It was time to go deeper.

"There are three issues in the public psyche that we have to attack, or we are undone," Dr. Soros said. "The first two are the Constitution and the truth. The media programming we will produce to defeat the Constitution and the notion of truth is not so difficult to engineer. We have been doing that for years. Let's be honest with ourselves that the truth does not serve our purposes. It is our enemy, in fact."

"The third item is the most difficult one for us. It is the most powerful emotional drive that human beings possess: Love. It is love that infuses our enemies with such great determination and vigor. You see, the Patriots love the old America: the One Nation Under God, Thanksgiving, Christmas, E. Pluribus Unum, apple pie and the Fourth of July. It is like a spiritual force in them, they love it so much. They want to live the American Dream again. These people *love* their country, and they want it back."

President Omeba looked at Dr. Soros with an angry scowl on his face.

"The Patriots love their country," the President remarked acidly. "That figures. I never did. It's not surprising, then, how bitter they are towards us," he said, turning in his chair and staring at the wall. "They get bitter, they cling to guns or religion or antipathy to people who aren't like them — or anti-immigrant sentiment, or anti-trade sentiment as a way to explain their frustrations. Their bitterness is what drives them to march up and down Pennsylvania Avenue and in state capitals all over the nation. Love makes them bitter towards us. You're right, Dr. Soros. Love is the main impediment to our agenda. It makes them tough and determined — and they all vote."

President Omeba turned in his chair to face the table again. Dr. Soros looked at him approvingly.

"It is more than the fact that they are bitter clingers," Soros said. "Their patriotic love of America makes them realize what they have lost — their liberty and freedom. They'll do anything to get the old America back."

Soros looked at the circle of frowning faces around the Situation Room conference table.

"What can we do about it?" Joe Bidet asked. "What about the truth? We have an outstanding legislative and policy record to stand on."

Dr. Soros shook his head in disgust. He had already decided that the Vice President was quite thick. But he did need to be diplomatic in his response.

"That depends on your point of view," Soros said. "At least half of the American people view you as traitors who should be tried and imprisoned for your crimes. Truth is of no use to the cause of international socialism. It never has been. The basis of socialist power is deception. With careful deception we can implant ignorance and fear in the minds of our subjects. We can control them with deception. We will make them fear and hate our political opposition. In order to do that we must keep the truth from the masses.

"No, Vice President Bidet," Dr. Soros said. He shook his head. "We cannot use the truth. The first casualty of war is truth. This is war. We cannot look back on the quaint notion of truth. It has no value to our revolution. Our agitprop must be carefully engineered and presented. There will be very little truth in it — just enough to make the rest seem plausible. I will write the President's speeches and he will read them using the teleprompter.

"President Omeba is the key. He has a great gift for speech-making. His oratorical skills and mesmerizing cadence will deliver our subliminal messages to the masses through the medium of television. We will brainstream our way to power."

14

GOING ROGUE

Colonel Plummer divided his forces after fleeing the Egyptians. He sent his dead and wounded to the CIA base in the desert, and took his remaining forces to a secret Mossad base on top of Mount Negev. They arrived in nine Blackhawk helicopters and a single Chinook, which dangled a nuclear bomb of Iranian manufacture in its cargo net. The militaries of six surrounding nations had put their military forces on full combat alert. They were searching for the mysterious military force that had attacked the Suez Canal. But Colonel Plummer's SpecOps team was concealed and secure in the Israeli intelligence base.

Colonel Plummer made a deal with the Israelis. He was not authorized to deliver the nuclear device to them, but it had to be done. Plummer understood that he could face court-martial for handing over the nuke. There would also be repercussions for blowing up the two supertankers and shutting down the Suez Canal, even though that was part of his mission plan. But the mission plan also included finding all of the Persian Bombs, and only two had been accounted for. The way Colonel Plummer saw it his mission was incomplete.

He developed a military plan of action and presented it to the Israelis. The Mossad saw the merit in his plan, and agreed to support his efforts to find the missing bomb. Plummer picked twenty of his best men to continue Operation Persian Bomb, which he would pursue with or without support from the American government and military. Plummer was going after the missing bomb, even if it meant going rogue.

The Turkish coffee was hot and strong. Joel Plummer welcomed its bracing effects, along with the hint of cardamom that gave the brew an exotic flavor. Moshe Argaman had made their coffees with honey and cream brought from a kibbutz in the far away land of milk and honey. They sat in wooden chairs at the top of Mount Negev and watched the sun slowly rise over the horizon. They were at the edge of the Makhtesh Ramon crater, high above the desert floor. It was the largest non-impact crater in the world, and the location of one of Mossad's top-secret military bases.

"I will leave the nuclear weapon with you," Colonel Plummer said. Moshe Argaman nodded his head and sipped his Turkish coffee.

"My government agrees to your proposal, and of course we accept the bomb," he said. "Now we have two Persian bombs."

"You got the other one?" Joel asked. "You have it in hand?"

"Yes. We captured it. Our losses were very heavy," Moshe replied. "It would have been easier if your government had not turned off the satellite imagery. It would have been easier if your military had actually provided the helicopter transport and commandos you promised us. Your withdrawal of support and forces just before the mission was...not taken well by our people."

Joel hung his head. To a soldier there was nothing more shameful than the act of abandoning the battlefield in the face of enemy fire. Abandoning a joint mission with an ally, and leaving the ally to fight alone, was the worst shame of all. It was beyond cowardly.

The blowback at the Pentagon — and with the Israeli Defense Forces — was very severe. Two-dozen top ranking American officers resigned their commissions in protest. The American/Israeli military alliance was shattered. The diplomatic aftermath was volcanic. But the Omeba administration turned a deaf ear to all objections to the executive order.

Three hundred Special Forces commandos en route to the Bekkah Valley were literally turned around in mid-air, and returned to their aircraft carrier. The Israelis received notice that the top-secret mission had been cancelled via a cable from the State Department. The American military was ordered to cease all communications with the Israeli military. The Israelis regarded the event as the most treacherous betrayal in their history.

Joel was mortified by what his government had done. He could not fathom any reason for cancelling American participation in the joint mission. His urgent satellite phone and radio calls to the Pentagon and to his CIA counterpart went unanswered. Joel Plummer and Seal Team Six were cut off. Isolated. As was Israel.

Plummer would have to improvise if he were to continue his mission and find that last bomb. So he made a deal with Moshe Argaman and the Israeli government to trade his captured nuke for logistical and military support. That alone could get him court-martialed and sent to Fort Leavenworth for life.

But there was still one bomb missing and it had to be found before the Iranians detonated it in a major city. Joel reminded the Israelis that the missing nuke just might be a second bomb designated for Israel. It was a possibility the Israelis could not ignore. Mahmoud Ahmanutjob had promised nuclear hellfire for the Jews on countless occasions.

It was also possible that the nuke was headed for Europe or the United States. The missing bomb had to be found and captured. Plummer proposed a joint military operation with the Mossad and the IDF. Colonel Plummer was a known quantity to the Israelis. They respected him and knew that he was a highly capable military commander. More than that, they felt that he could be trusted. After a night of internal consultation and debate, with strong input from Moshe Argaman, the Israeli government agreed to Plummer's proposal.

The Mossad had operated observation posts from the Makhtesh Ramon area for decades, and recently upgraded the base as an intelligence-gathering center and to provide a platform to hunt terrorist infiltrators. The rocky expanse was far from civilization. People did not live in the Negev Desert, except for a few hard-scrabble nomadic tribes. It was too harsh a place for modern people to live.

The American Special Forces commander and the Mossad agent sipped their coffee and watched as the new day began. They had much to ponder. The Suez Canal was closed to shipping. The two VLCC supertankers Colonel Plummer had grounded and blown up were still burning furiously. Diplomatic channels around the world were overloaded with traffic and dire posturing. The benchmark price of crude oil had skyrocketed overnight and continued a steep climb.

"I'm glad you got the Bekkah Valley bomb," Colonel Plummer said. "That's a huge load off my mind. Now we can focus all our efforts on finding the last device."

"Yes," Moshe agreed. He took a sip of his coffee. The cardamom spice was strong. "Now we are in possession of *two* Persian Bombs. There is a popular opinion among my countrymen that we should return both of them to the Iranians."

Plummer found the thought amusing and alarming at the same time. It would be ironic if the Iranian's own nuclear bombs were detonated in *their* major cities. But the consequences would be disastrous.

"That would start World War III," he said.

"Yes. But Israel would not have to worry about the Persians for a long time. And we can take care of the Egyptians and the rest of the Arabs if we have to. It will be difficult but we can do it. As long as Turkey does not enter the fighting, Israel can hold off the Mohammedans."

"How about China?"

"No chance of China getting involved in the Middle East."

"There is a chance. Major General Zhang Zhaozdong said that the Chinese army would protect Iran even at the risk of a third world war."

"I heard about that. Zhaozdong is a drama queen. Do you think there is any substance to the threat?"

"Yes. I do. China needs oil. If the Chinese Navy were to appear off Haifa, I don't think the current administration would do much to aid Israel."

"They would not," Argaman agreed. "Your President is a Muslim. Muslims hate Jews as a matter of course. We no longer look to the United States as a friend and ally. We see your present government as an enemy."

The statement was a shock to Plummer. But Plummer didn't doubt that the Israeli military viewed America very differently after the Bekkah Valley debacle. He couldn't blame them.

"Americans are not your enemy," Joel said. He never thought he'd have to say such a thing to an Israeli.

"I know that," Moshe said softly. "But your government can no longer be trusted."

Joel had no argument to that. The men sipped their Turkish coffee and looked into the desert. The sun peeked above the horizon, sending streaks of light across the rugged brown terrain.

"One bomb in Tel Aviv would mean the end of Israel," Moshe said abstractly.

"Yes. It probably would," Joel agreed. "But why wouldn't they bomb Jerusalem? That would be the harshest blow anyone could strike against the Jews."

"It's the Dome of the Rock," Moshe replied. "The Muslims erected their shrine on our temple mount for a reason, and that was to prevent the temple from being rebuilt. But now they can't destroy Jerusalem because of that cursed dome: it has become a holy of holies for them. The legend, you see, is that Mohammed rose into heaven from the temple mount."

"I know the legend. But I thought Mohammed never left Saudi Arabia."

"He didn't," Moshe said. "But in Islam they say he was called to heaven by Allah, and that he went up to heaven from the site of Solomon's Temple in Israel. It's a curiosity, to say the least. Yes. According to the Muslims, Mohammed rode a white horse from the Temple Mount in Jerusalem into heaven. The name of the horse was Barak."

Joel looked at Moshe in astonishment.

"You've got to be kidding me."

"I wish I were, my friend."

They sat in silence for long minutes. The sun rose slowly, casting dark shadows behind the tall rocks of the Negev. The land was broken and bleak in the vicinity of Makhtesh Ramon. It was a wasteland. Joel heard a shrill cry in the distance, some kind of bird. He remembered a fable told him by an Israeli commando many years ago. There was a large flightless bird in the Negev that was to be avoided at all cost. It had poison quills that it could shoot at you. If a quill struck you, then you would die a long and painful death. There was no cure.

The Negev was filled with myths like that. The reality of their situation, however, was much worse than any desert fable. Many people would die horribly if the Persian Bomb got away from them and out into the world. That was not a myth.

Joel found himself deep in thought. He rarely thought of a desert as being beautiful. They were sterile deadly places. But watching sunrise in the Negev from atop the desert mountain brought out deep feelings in him. He found himself in a state of awe.

"The Light of the World cometh," he whispered.

The Jew looked over at him, astonished. Israelis were often surprised at the effect their homeland had on visiting Christians. But he understood exactly what his friend meant by his remark. It had nothing to do with the sun.

The Sayeret Matkal was an IDF Special Forces unit attached to the Israeli intelligence unit, AMAN. Their prime functions were intelligence gathering and commando operations deep inside enemy territory.

When Colonel Joel Plummer took his Special Forces team rogue to track the remaining Iranian nuclear device, he had no idea that his operation would receive top priority mission support from Israel's premier intelligence force. He had dealt with Mossad for many years, and was comfortable working with Moshe and his organization. The Sayeret Matkal was something completely different. It was dangerous, powerful and beyond any law.

Once Moshe Argaman explained the arrangements that had been made on his behalf, Plummer realized the depth of the Israeli commitment to his mission. The Israelis were giving him their best intelligence assets and military forces to track down the remaining bomb. They were giving him everything they had at a time when Israel desperately needed all of its resources focused on protecting Israel.

The Sayeret Matkal had deep sources and relationships inside the Pentagon and at CIA headquarters in Langley, Virginia. Plummer learned that several American military and civilian security agencies were secretly operating in defiance of the executive directives from the White House.

Plummer's team was not alone. Others understood the threat of an Iranian nuclear bomb and were willing to risk everything to neutralize that threat. The Pentagon and the CIA secretly deployed top-level intelligence assets to aid Colonel Plummer and the Israeli commando forces. The Omeba administration was kept in the dark.

Each government fielded six independent commando teams to find and capture the missing nuclear weapon. Colonel Plummer's commando team was code-named 'Daniel'. Their objective: the twenty-kiloton nuclear warhead code-named 'The Prince of Persia'.

The two governments put more than a thousand agents and operatives in the field to hunt for the weapon. Intelligence reports began to trickle in almost immediately. The Sayeret Matkal acted as control. The Pentagon could not risk any leakage or exposure to their own civilian administration. The CIA, however, had resources even Leon Panera knew nothing about.

All of the preliminary intelligence reports proved to be misleading. The Iranians had sent multiple decoy teams out with fake bomb packages to lead investigators astray. This tactic worked. But it revealed the absolute determination of the Iranians to detonate their nuclear warheads on their selected targets. The Americans were astonished at the level of cunning and technical sophistication displayed by the Iranians. The Israelis were not.

The Sayeret Matkal and the Mossad had preliminary intelligence on the origin and transport of the three nuclear bombs. They were manufactured at Nantaz, five hundred miles south of the holy city of Qom. The devices were ordinary enriched uranium-235 core devices, with conventional chemical explosive detonators. Each weighed one thousand kilograms and had a blast yield of twenty kilotons. The three devices were loaded into separate commercial trucks. Each bomb truck had two decoy trucks and covert paramilitary forces from the Iranian National Guard to escort them.

One truck left Nantaz in the dead of night on a long overland journey through southern Iran. The bomb and escort trucks crossed the Iraqi border, drove through Baghdad, Al-Ramadi and Ar Rutba. The Persian Bomb then crossed the Syrian border, where it was lost to American satellites and Sayeret Matkal humint sources for two days.

In a stroke of luck, the truck was detained at the Lebanese border crossing near Qaa, which the CIA learned by monitoring Syrian military computer traffic. Sayeret Matkal field agents spotted the truck, confirmed the presence of radioactive emissions, and mounted a GPS tracking device on it. They had located the first of the Persian Bombs — the one targeted for Tel Aviv.

From the Lebanese border, the truck was tracked by satellite and GPS and trailed overland by Israeli agents. They followed the truck to a Hamas training camp in the heart of the Bekkah Valley, deep inside Lebanon.

The second Persian Bomb was loaded onto a truck and hauled directly to Bandar Ganaveh on the Iranian coast. There it was loaded onto an Iranian Navy engineering barge, and transported to the Kargh Island petroleum terminal. From there it was loaded into the forward petroleum compartment of an Iranian Tanker Company VLCC oil tanker. The bomb travelled with a decoy tanker into the Suez Canal. That is where Colonel Plummer and Seal Team Six found them. Intelligence sources indicated that this bomb was targeted for New York City.

The third Iranian nuke was still missing. No trace of it could be found until twelve days after Operation Persian Bomb had begun. This bomb was also placed on a commercial truck and carried in a direction no one was expecting.

The device had taken the long surface roads north, and then west, from Iran and through Turkey. Its current location was uncertain, but the best intelligence guess was that the missing Persian Bomb, the Prince of Persia, was en route to the ancient city of Tarsus. Israeli intelligence speculated that the device was going to be transported across the Mediterranean Sea to a European city, but there was no evidence to support the speculation. The current location and ultimate destination of the Prince of Persia remained unknown.

15

BRAVE NEW WORLD

Amassive crowd of protesters swarmed the streets, sidewalks and grounds outside the White House. A constant stream of them paraded up and down both sides of Pennsylvania Avenue with their banners and picket signs. Some were dressed in Revolutionary War period costumes, some were in business suits, and many wore jeans and tee shirts. There was a Betsy Ross who waved a flag that had a circle of thirteen stars over a blue background with thirteen stripes. George Washington and Abe Lincoln walked together in deep conversation. Ben Franklin gabbed with a group of tittering young women in Civil War hoop skirts. Paul Revere cantered along on his horse shouting, "The Zombies are coming! The Zombies are coming!"

The vast majority of the protesters identified themselves as Patriots. While they shared many of the ideals and goals of the Tea Party, they weren't inclined to join an organized political movement.

They were ordinary Americans who woke up one day to find that their country had been taken over by the socialist elite. The Patriots had no political organization, nor had any aspirations for one. They just wanted their country back. And they were willing to fight for it. They came from everywhere.

The Tea Party had thousands of people in the streets that day, carrying signs and operating information booths. They provided most of the written material for distribution, and had a visible political organization, with leaders giving speeches and haranguing the crowds. Many of the marchers paraded with Gladsten flags: a coiled rattlesnake on a yellow background, with 'Don't Tread on Me' emblazoned beneath the poisonous serpent. Many protesters wore the tricorn, three-cornered hats. Mothers with children were everywhere. The people marched, sang patriotic songs and waved their signs and banners, while their children ran excitedly through the throng. The crowd was polite and calm, happy to be with other patriots. But they were obviously unhappy with the government in power, the object of their protest.

President Omeba watched them with growing wonder and contempt. The Inner Circle was with him: Joe Bidet, Rahm Adramelech, Valerie Garrotte, Eric Holdup, Janet Napolitburo, Tim Geitmare and Gay Carney. Dr. Soros had also joined them. All watched the crowd on the Situation Room monitors.

The protesters had been growing in numbers every day. Pennsylvania Avenue had become a barometer of the nation's mood. The more it filled up with protesters, the higher the tension in the newsrooms and government offices. The President's staff experienced a sense of dread that grew in direct proportion to the number of protesters parading outside the White House. At any given time, there were half a million of them, night and day. The

President had become obsessed with the protestors. They represented a direct threat to his administration — to his ego.

"I don't see what they're getting all wee wee'd up about," Omeba said. "Is it the taxes? It's not like they've got anything better to do with their money. Accusing me of using a socialist mop!"

He slammed his palm down hard on the conference table.

"I don't get this tax thing," Omeba complained. "These Tea Baggers, or whatever they are, think they're so cute playing Boston Tea Party. They're pissing me off. They think they're taxed enough already? They haven't seen anything yet. I'm just getting *started* spreading the wealth around."

Valerie was beginning to worry about him. He was working himself up to one of his raving fits.

"Just look at those people out there!" he demanded of his Inner Circle.

Some of them strained their necks for a better look at the closed circuit monitors.

"What kind of signs are they carrying anyway? Look at that *fool*," Omeba said, pointing to a tall thin fellow with a black stovepipe hat, and a sign he was carrying.

"'Down with *Tranny?*' Look at that sign that fool is carrying. This is outrageous! Those bigots actually want to outlaw being a tranny? When being a transvestite becomes outlawed, I'm for overthrowing that government and establishing a society where same sex relationships are not frowned upon. And men can wear dresses when they want to!"

"What on earth are you talking about?" Rahm asked.

"Hate crimes and discrimination against transsexuals."

"No. It must be about something else." Rahm squinted to get a better look at the signs and protesters in the monitor.

"This isn't about sexual orientation?" Omeba replied.

"No. It's about tyranny. These people are saying *you're* a tyrant!"

"Well that's ridiculous. I've never worn a dress in public. Look at the signs they're carrying outside! 'Down with Trannys!' What kind of sick people are they anyway?"

"Its 'Down with *Tyrants*', sir," Rahm said.

"Oh."

The President was agitated. The protesters were having a very negative affect on his poll ratings, and he was plenty worried about it. It was evident to everyone that the protesters must be done away with. Rahm and Valerie turned to Dr. Soros. They brought him back into the picture to help get rid of the growing dissent, and he had been busy at work generating the subliminal messaging intended to modify the behavior of the American people. But all it seemed to be doing was stirring up the Patriots and Tea Partiers.

"Well, Dr. Soros," Rahm said, leaning forward. "As you can see...matters have not improved."

Soros replied in a precise, calculated tone.

"I have studied the situation, compiled data, and conducted an exhaustive analysis of the alternatives. We have conducted some brainstreaming trials to see if we could get the protestors to go home, or at least calm them down a bit. Unfortunately, these people are resistant to television indoctrination."

"Well..." Valerie said. She was clearly not happy with his response. "How about the re-election programming then. Are we making any progress?"

"Alas, no," Winfrey Soros said. "The prospects for re-election are not good either. It could be too late to do *anything*."

"What are you talking about?" Valerie countered. "We have an approval rating of forty percent. We can build on that. We only need to gain another fifteen or twenty percent to capture the two hundred and seventy electoral votes we need. We can do that on negative campaigning alone. We haven't got that far to go to catch up. I have to disagree with you, Dr. Soros."

"You have much farther to go than you think," Soros replied. "The problem is that people are waking up. It's like the old joke about the puppies."

Valerie rounded on Soros. "Puppy joke? I haven't heard that one."

"For the purpose of making my point, I will tell the joke," Dr. Soros said. "This boy is selling puppies outside the White House. He has a sign that says 'Democrat Puppies For Sale.' President Bill Clitman walks by and the boy yells out to him 'Hey Mister, you want to buy a Democrat puppy?' The President looks into the boy's box at the cute puppies but declines and walks away. That night he tells Hillary the amusing story about the boy selling cute Democrat puppies, and she says that they should buy one for the White House. So the next morning Bill and Hillary walk out to the sidewalk and are very pleased to see the boy still there selling puppies. But his sign now reads 'Republican Puppies for Sale.' Bill Clitman says, 'Now, young man. I was here yesterday and you were advertising *Democrat* puppies for sale. These are the same puppies. What's the deal?' The boy replies, 'Yes sir. They're the same puppies. But that was *yesterday.* Today they have their eyes open."

Joe Bidet broke into loud guffawing laughter and pounded the table. He thought the joke was hysterically funny. No one else did. Not in the least. They fully understood the point Dr. Soros just made. It was quite an insult. They looked at Dr. Soros with irritation and suspicion; a few of them were beginning to wonder which side of the fence he was working.

"I hope you can understand and appreciate what I'm telling you. I know it is difficult to hear," Dr. Soros said. "I told you the same thing the last time we met. The American people have opened their eyes. They are on to you. They see through you. They have had enough of you. That is why the entire nation is on the march. You had better take corrective measures before it's too late. It might already be too late."

The room was quiet. Everyone was thinking the same thing. It was time to update the resume. Quite possibly Dr. Soros was right and the game was up.

"Nonsense!" Omeba said at last. He looked everyone squarely in the eyes. His expression was classically arrogant Barak Hussein Omeba. He sneered at them.

"I can do anything I want," the President said, "I can say anything I want and they'll believe me."

"Don't you go getting a big head, Barry," Valerie cautioned. She recognized that narcissistic imperious gleam in his eye.

"Valerie...remember during the campaign how wildly they cheered when I blew my nose on stage?"

"Yeah. That was pretty weird."

"They loved it. The applause I got for that beat anything I said up to that point."

"That's 'cause your nose blow made more sense," she replied. "You weren't using the teleprompter back then, Barry."

"You're all *forgetting* something," Omeba said, shaking his finger at them. "We have *me*. I just need to go out and give speeches. I just need to be audacious again. *Yes we can!* People loved that one. Even *Hope and Change* still has some mileage left in it. We're *Winning the Future*! See? All we need are some snappy new campaign slogans, and me speaking endlessly and getting a lot of TV coverage. The people just need to see me...listen to me speak."

The Inner Circle all looked at him. There was a time when his rousing pep talks would have gotten their blood pumping. In times past, they would have jumped on top of the conference table and danced with joy, certain that he had come up with another brilliant solution to whatever insurmountable problem faced them. But over time, one by one, each of his closest advisors had come to the conclusion that he was highly overrated; that he was not a brilliant thinker; that, in fact, he had no idea what he was doing. They saw through him too. And at that moment each of them realized that Dr. Soros was absolutely correct. A large part of the American populace had opened their eyes. They weren't Democrat puppies any more.

The American people finally realized that Lush Rimshot, Ben Gleck and Han Sanity had been right about Barak Hussein Omeba all along. Omeba wasn't a genius light worker: he was a radical Marxist who was determined to impose socialist government on the American people. And they were fed up with him.

His closest supporters looked at Omeba with uncertain eyes, revealing their growing concern. Did he still have the magic? Could he still pull off their utopian dream? Or was the hope and change he promised merely hype and shortchange?

He sat there smiling back at them, as if he expected them to *get* it at any moment. Surely they must see that he was anointed for this great task; that he was truly The One. This was all about him, after all.

Vice President Bidet turned to Dr. Soros.

"What can we do, Dr. Soros?" he pleaded. "What can we do?"

The good doctor looked at each of them in turn.

"What is your current reelection strategy?" the internet media mogul asked.

Valerie perked up at this. This was her baby. She had personally developed the high-impact reelection strategy.

"Our election strategy is four-fold," she said. "We're going to focus on the professional white vote. We own the minorities, homosexuals and unions. We own the government workers. Our weakness is in the independents. Without the professional white voter we're toast. But we know how to get to them.

"First, we claim the Republicans are determined to destroy the middle class. We offer proof, and we beat them up on that really hard. Second, we claim that the economy is in good shape. That's a tougher sell, but we've already begun to work on some of the jobs numbers and other statistics. Third, we accuse the opposing candidate of having sexual affairs. It doesn't matter who our Republican opponent is. We make the claims, produce a few bimbos that have a shelf life longer than the news cycle, and it'll be good enough. Forth, we label them as racist. If we can successfully label them as racist, then we will win. Look what we did to the Tea Party."

"You think this will work? This racist labeling?" Dr. Soros asked. "Frankly, I think the American people are wise to that by now. You have been crying race wolf ever since election day."

"If we can tar them by calling them racist, nobody will want anything to do with them," Valerie replied.

"But they're *not* racist," Vice President Bidet said. "I've worked with the Republicans longer than anybody here. I've worked with them for decades. They aren't racist. Tea Partiers aren't either. Heck, they aren't half as racist as the Democratic Party. Compared to the NAACP, the Tea Partiers are completely non-racist."

The Inner Circle collectively closed their eyes and braced for the backlash from Adramelech. Joe Bidet never missed a meeting without saying something unbelievably stupid. When Rahm didn't yell at Joe, everyone relaxed. Then President Omeba spoke up.

"They're racist if *I* say they are," he said. "There's truthiness to the idea of our political opponents being racist. The truth is what we say it is. If our entire party says the Republican candidate is racist, then the media will pick up the meme. They'll dig up proof even if they have to forge it. Witnesses won't be a problem. Just make sure that the women they're having affairs with aren't black. They're racists. We win."

Joe Bidet looked reluctant to go along with the idea. Something about this tactic didn't sit well with him. Rahm Adramelech was fine with it, however.

"I like the strategy, Valerie," Rahm said. " He who defines the terms controls the debate. And he who controls the debate, controls the outcome. We'll have the alphabet soup media define the Republicans as racist for us — and they'll just shrivel up. I know these guys. This is their Achilles heel. I just wish we had a really good crisis we could throw into the mix. A good crisis would work for us."

"Our political opponents are racist by definition," Omeba declared. "If they oppose *me*...then they're *racist*."

This was so patently obvious to the liberal mentality that no one questioned it. Valerie smiled at the President. She gave him her special wink. He needed assurance. He craved it. She could tell.

"You are so right, Mr. President," Valerie said. She reached across the table and patted his hand. "Right as usual. Good thing the bimbo eruption got rid of Randy Cain. That was excellent work, Rahm. We took the Tea Party's black candidate out from under them. It's time to play hardball with these Repugs. They bring a knife....we bring a gun."

The President's advisors congratulated one another for a few minutes. One by one they heaped praise on President Omeba. He needed it. They all could tell. Dr. Soros looked at them doubtfully. It was obvious that he was not satisfied with the reelection strategy. There was obviously something else he wanted to say. They looked at him expectantly. Finally he spoke up.

"The four strategies you just outlined won't be enough," he said. "You need to do more and you need to do it immediately — before those crowds outside start doing something themselves. Something serious. I said that President Omeba's reelection would be difficult. I did not say it would be impossible. But to succeed we need to go beyond these ordinary political measures you are discussing. We need to use drastic measures. It is time to go nuclear."

They pondered his words. Omeba was first to speak.

"Anything," President Omeba said to the psychoengineer billionaire. "Whatever it takes."

The others nodded in agreement. Dr. Soros looked long and hard at Omeba. At length he was satisfied the President meant what he had just said. The President was ready for extraordinary measures.

"It is time for conflict. We must stir up dissatisfaction and discontent," Dr. Soros said coldly. Rahm leaned forward to listen more closely. "President Omeba, you have developed a massive power base — the progressive zombies. They are an army. It is time to deploy them. Power is not only what you have, but what the enemy thinks you have.

"Your first strategy to make hobgoblins out of the Republicans by saying they are a threat to the middle class is a good one. Class warfare is the essence of socialist struggle. Hatred of the bourgeoisie must be exploited. President Omeba will rescue the people from the hobgoblin capitalists. This is good.

"Your second strategy of claiming that the economy is actually in good shape is risky, but positive. You must promote the fear that if the Republicans gain the White House, then the economy will get worse. Fear is our friend.

"The third strategy of accusing your opponents of having sexual affairs seems weak to me. But I do understand it will cause divisions in the Republican ranks, so that is good. Make the enemy live up to it's own set of rules. They can never do that. Nobody can.

"Your fourth strategy of declaring your political opponents as being racists is brilliant. Pick the target, freeze it, personalize it, and polarize it. Branding the Patriots, the Tea Partiers and Republicans, as racists will destroy them. They will freeze like deer in the headlights, unable to save themselves. Paint them with the racist label and the nation will be divided to our advantage."

Dr. Soros paused to deliver his coup de grace. He looked at each of them carefully.

"Once all that is done, we will have successfully divided the nation along class, racial and ideological lines. Then we must add the element of conflict. Conflict with the prevailing patterns will change those patterns so that we can shape them to our purpose. We must keep the people in conflict with one another, and with their beliefs. This is the strategy that will succeed for you, President Omeba. This is the strategy that will advance our glorious cause. We must plunge America into turmoil and conflict.

"*You* must do this, President Omeba. You are the only one who can. This moment in history is yours to seize. You must tell your followers to rise up and revolt against their capitalist overlords. It is time for the proletariat to throw off the shackles of the bourgeoisie. Workers of the world unite!"

The Inner Circle cheered wildly.

16

WASHINGTON TEA PARTY

President Omeba gave barnburner political speeches for an entire week. Non-stop. Every day. Several times each day. The effect on the nation was electrifying. Gavin Bond, the BBC news correspondent, monitored the speeches and studied the effects they had on the American people. He was amazed at what was happening in the former colonies. The entire nation was stirred up. It was in a frenzied state; kept there by a constant stream of provocative political messages and incendiary attacks from the White House.

President Omeba's speeches galvanized his supporters and hardened his enemies. The speeches were clearly meant to be divisive, and he held forth with powerful delivery. Omeba's language was fiery and accusatory. His rhetoric had never soared so high. His excoriation of those who opposed him had never been more brutal or more personal — even defaming individuals and organizations, and inviting his followers to harass and persecute them. His worst invective was reserved for the retrogressive reactionaries he called The Patriots.

But while his soaring speeches and malignant rhetoric unified his zombies and mobilized his political allies, they had the opposite effect on those who opposed him. His opponents were furious with his false accusations and slanderous misrepresentations concerning them. They were outraged at being called racist, and being accused of stealing from the poor. They too were galvanized to action: The Patriots wanted to throw President Omeba out of office. They couldn't wait to evict him from the White House. *'We Can't Wait — Out Now!'* became a major theme of signs and banners carried by White House protesters. The fragile fiction of American unity was shattered asunder; polarized along political, class and racial lines. All according to plan.

Gavin Bond didn't want to believe that the American President was deliberately trying to set the nation at war against itself, but he could not deny that the partisan propaganda and ugly polemic from the White House was having precisely that effect. It was as if the President was intentionally creating conflict among the people.

The rest of the world watched events in the United States with amazement and fear. America was no longer the leader of the free world. America was no longer the leader of anything. It was corrupt. It was broke. It could not govern itself. Other peoples of the world stopped laughing at America once they realized that the nation was truly falling apart right before their eyes. It was only then that they began to contemplate a world without the United States as a stabilizing force for good and for world peace.

Gavin and his crew filed two or three reports each day. Gavin was covering the biggest news story of the century: the meltdown and destruction of the United States of America. Bond knew the Americans well. He even thought he understood them. But for the life of him, he found it difficult to believe what the Americans were doing to one another. The United States was tearing itself apart.

He held the forlorn hope that the nation would come to its senses at the last minute and save itself. This was possible. The Americans were not like Europeans who, centuries ago, had accepted their fate as peons ruled by an elite class. The Americans would stand up. They would fight. At least this was the hope that Gavin harbored in his heart.

Gavin Bond's BBC production crew was in high demand. They discovered that they had easy access to just about anyone they wanted to interview. In Washington, D.C., in particular, they found that their BBC credentials — and Gavin Bond's reputation — got them carte blanche entry to the highest levels of government. After the first week of work, Gavin knew why it was so easy for him to get interviews with top administration officials. The administration wanted to use the BBC as part of its ongoing national propaganda campaign.

With one exception, the American television news media were all in for the Omeba administration, and acted eagerly as propaganda conduits. The alphabet soup mainstream networks worked openly as Democratic Party operatives, spouting the four talking points of class warfare, the good economy, sexual improprieties of the Republican and Tea Party officials, and cries of racism against all white people, and even against people of color, if they stood up to defend whites or did not toe the party line.

Ordinarily the BBC, and all of the European news organizations would automatically support progressive administrations and criticize conservative ones. But this time, Gavin knew that he had to report the actual truth of the matter at hand. He could not show the usual liberal media bias that was so ingrained in him. The usual course of action would be improper under the circumstances. The story he was covering was of supreme importance to everyone in the world. His reportage would become part of history. Gavin believed that the United States was on the brink of a second civil war.

Gavin decided to conduct his own investigations into the extraordinary changes that were overtaking America, and to present an objective series of stories for BBC and American viewers, and for posterity. This was the story of the century and he wanted to get it right.

Gavin Bond left Washington, D.C., the belly of the beast, and travelled across America to find the essence and truth of the story. It was unfolding everywhere he went. The whole of America was being torn apart with class warfare, racist polarization, lurid slander involving sexual improprieties, and bizarre government statements in clear opposition to the facts.

The BBC correspondent and his crew bypassed Omeba's political propagandists in government and the media, and went to schools and universities to speak directly to the American people. They interviewed workers and management at large factories, they cadged random people on the streets, and questioned them as to what they believed was happening. They spoke with church leaders and bus drivers and airline pilots. They recorded loud arguments on street corners and witnessed violent clashes between competing marchers and protesters.

Gavin travelled across the nation for two weeks to find the truth of the situation. He soon discovered that the story at its roots was a struggle for the soul of the nation. The American people were fighting among themselves not only to define the future political course of the nation, but more importantly, to define what it meant to be an American.

The driving force of the conflict was so very familiar to Gavin: international socialism and its perpetual revolutionary struggle to destroy capitalism. It was the story of the strife between the haves and the have-nots, between those who believed in individual property rights, and those who believed in collectivism. It was the fight between those who believed in freedom and liberty against those who were certain that the masses must be ruled by the central authority of the state and governed by an enlightened elite.

For the first time in his life, Gavin realized that he had been working for the wrong side of the debate; that his heart and mind longed for the freedom and liberty of the old America, and not the progressive socialism of the European state.

If the progressives succeeded, America would no longer be the land of truth, liberty and justice. America would eventually succumb to communism, under which the individual looked to the government for everything, including his ethics and morality. God and the Ten Commandments would have no place in Progressive America. Neither would the Constitution and the Bill of Rights.

The Omeba administration intended to be transformational. President Omeba said so publicly and on many occasions. His administration planned to sweep away two hundred and thirty years of American tradition, values and Constitutional government, and replace it with a socialist state dedicated to Marxist theory and practice. That much had become clear in the steady propaganda that emanated from the White House, federal government offices and the mainstream media.

Gavin and his BBC crew returned to Washington, D.C. They were amazed at the throngs that flooded the downtown area. The rental van had to be parked miles away, and the walk to the center of power was a long one.

Gavin mixed in with a crowd of Tea Partiers parading up and down Pennsylvania Avenue to interview them. Gavin and his crew were initially met with hostile looks and words: the news media were the enemy of the American people. Everyone knew that. But his British accent and charming ways softened the Americans and they spoke with him freely and openly. There were so many interesting looking people it was difficult to select the best to interview.

His impression of Tea Partiers and Patriots was completely different from that portrayed by the American news media. They were not uneducated. They were *highly* educated, most of them. They were certainly not racist. Their black members ate and camped with all the others, and nobody thought to make a big deal about it. The African Americans had an equal voice in everything. The Tea Partiers were not sexist either. Nearly half of the Tea Party protesters were women, who were pretty and bright and had a firm grasp of the issues that brought them to Pennsylvania Avenue.

Gavin and his crew passed among the protesters and recorded their stories. One of the protest leaders railed loudly on progressive politics for Gavin's benefit, as he walked by a large decorated booth. Gavin passed him by. He wanted to speak with the people — not the leaders. He felt a tug at his sleeve. He looked at the man who wanted his attention.

"You can't trust a damn liberal," an old Army veteran said to him. From his boonie hat and O.D. garb, Gavin gathered that the old man was a veteran of the Vietnam War.

"All the liberals ever do is lie!" the old man said.

A young, Asian-looking college student standing nearby agreed, "At no time is the Omeba administration not lying to us. They lie constantly...always...about everything. There is no truth in them."

"Yeah," the veteran agreed. "And they screw up everything they touch. Everything liberals get involved in turns to shit. You know?"

"Yes," Gavin found himself agreeing. "It's the Labor Party in my country. Every single one of their darling programs has failed and bankrupted the treasury. Nothing they do ever works out. Our Labor Party and your Democratic Party seem very much alike."

"You have conservatives?"

"We call them Lords."

"You really call them that?"

"Well...yes, we do."

"They ever any trouble to you?"

"Yes. They are. Not as bad as the Laborites, who seemed determined to tear down the country and destroy our culture. Both parties are a nuisance."

"Sounds like we got a lot in common," the old veteran said. "But *we* have the First Amendment."

"Yes, that's free speech," Gavin said. "We don't have that one. It isn't permitted in Europe. The governments own and control the mass media."

"They control ours too now. That's why we got the *second* amendment."

"Ah yes! The guns. The right to keep and bear them."

"And the right to shoot them at polecat politicians when they've stepped over the line."

"Do you really plan to shoot politicians?"

"Mister Englishman from the BBC," the old veteran said. "You just take a look around you at what's going on in this country. The liberals control the government. They control the media. They control our education system. And they've got about half our population completely brainwashed. Our political system is corrupt and broke. They lie to us constantly. They tax and spend us into poverty and debt. The elections are rife with voter fraud. They don't listen to us anyway. We don't have representative government anymore. Does this sound familiar to you, Mr. Englishman? What do they expect us to do? What did *King George* expect us to do?"

"Ah...well...there you go," Gavin said. He looked sideways at the cameraman and received a thumbs-up. They got the whole conversation. It would be on the BBC network, and all over the world, later that evening. Gavin Bond was in a video clip gold mine. He thanked the Vietnam veteran and went digging for more.

He didn't have to go far. He found an attractive young mother carrying a large sign that said 'The Only Way to Cut Spending is to Cut Democrats!' It seemed to be a popular sentiment. She had a forward papoose with a tiny baby sleeping on her chest, and a four-year old boy trailing behind her, blowing noisily into a toy fife.

"Oh Miss?" Gavin greeted. "Might I have a word with you?"

"Sure...Mr....um. What news agency are you with?"

"BBC, Ma'am. I'm Gavin Bond. My cameraman is Ian Anderson. He plays the flute too," he said, nodding to the boy. "I'm curious about your sign. Do you really blame the Democratic Party for your government's excessive spending?"

The young woman brushed a strand of brunette hair from her face and looked at Gavin as if he was demented.

"Well...*duh*!" she said. "The Democratic Party started the socialist programs with the New Deal under FDR. Lamedim Braines Johnson kicked them into high gear in the nineteen sixties with his Great Society program. And after Carper, Clitman and now Omeba — and sixty years of Democrat-controlled Congresses — government spending is completely out of control. Did you know that in just three years, Barry Hussein Omeba added over one and a half *trillion* dollars to the annual deficit, and over five *trillion* dollars to the national debt? In just three years? That is absolutely insane."

"Why yes," Gavin said, turning to make sure Ian got his good side. "But Europe is doing the same thing. The social spending — your nation calls it entitlement spending — has burst budgets and sent governments into debt all over Europe, too."

"Who cares what Europe is doing?" the young woman retorted. "They're hardly setting an example anyone should follow. Socialism, communism and Nazism all came from Europe. Europe can kiss my grits!"

"Ah well...your grits is it?" Gavin said. "You might recall that the Magna Carta also came from Europe."

"So did the Bubonic Plague," the woman said. "So did World Wars I and II. So will World War III. We've had a *belly* full of Europe. That's why we left Europe in the first place. We want our liberty back."

"Is that why you've taken the time away from your life...away from motherhood to come here today to protest?"

Gavin gave his cameraman a subtle signal to zoom in on the woman's face for her response.

"I came here today to protest so that my children will have a future," she said. "The Democrats have spent us twenty trillion dollars into debt. Do you know how much money that is? My children's, children's grandchildren won't be able to pay it off. We have to stop the Democrats if we hope to *have* a future. Take a look at my sign, Mister BBC. The only way to cut spending is to cut Democrats! We have to cut Democrats if our children are to have any kind of future at all!"

"Ah yes. Well then. Thank you very much. You've given our viewers much to think about."

Gavin bowed away from the woman, giddy with the content he was collecting for his broadcasts. He was in a sound bite treasure house, and it was panning out spectacularly. He looked around for his next subject. It walked up to him.

The man was middle-aged and black. He wore an Uncle Sam outfit, complete with red and white striped pants, a blue jacket, a red bow tie, and a top hat with stars on it. The man had a white goatee glued to his chin and he was grinning from ear to ear.

"Gavin Bond," the black man greeted. "I'm Uncle Sam. I've seen you on TV. Mostly in England, but you're well known."

"Why...thank you," Gavin said. He was somewhat taken aback that someone in the crowd would know who he was. Generally, only effete liberal urban dwellers knew his work — not the average American. Certainly not right-wing patriot types.

"Pleased to meet you...er, Uncle Sam," Gavin said. "Are you a Tea Party member?"

"Of course I am. I'm very proud to be a Tea Partier."

"Well...it's sort of unusual isn't it? You being black and all. Not many African-Americans in the Tea Party, I understand."

Uncle Sam looked at Gavin sadly.

"There are a lot of patriotic black Tea Party members. Asians, Hispanics and Indians too," Uncle Sam said. "To tell you the truth, I feel a lot safer when I'm with Tea Partiers than when I'm anywhere else in American society."

"Why is that?"

"Well, it's because they're all law abiding citizens. They love this country. They understand the Constitution and what it stands for: liberty and justice for all. That means *all* of us, no matter what color you are. I haven't met a racist in the Tea Party yet — and I don't expect to."

"That's not the Tea Party's reputation," Gavin said.

"You mean that's not the propaganda that streams from the alphabet media and the Democratic Party. They call anyone who disagrees with them racist bigots. Nobody with any sense pays attention to those people. I certainly don't."

"Why are you a Tea Partier?" Gavin asked, raising his microphone. "Why are you here protesting today? Why the Uncle Sam getup?"

"It's real simple, Gavin," the black man said, smiling. "We Tea Partiers love our country. We love everything about it. We love our Constitution and our Bill of Rights. We love our heritage and culture. But we've been under heavy attack by cultural and political Marxists for decades now. Political correctness and cultural diversity are killing us. We've got to stand up and fight for our country. We don't want to see it go socialist. That's what this is all about. Most conflicts these days are about the same thing. There's an international cold war being waged between socialism and capitalism. America has been the land of opportunity and justice, and has done more good for its own folks and others in the world, *because* of our capitalist economic system. Thank God for capitalism. God Bless America!"

Gavin never took his eyes off the black Uncle Sam in front of him. He was fascinated by him. It was obvious the man was speaking his heart-felt convictions.

"Let me ask you a question, Mr. BBC," Uncle Sam said. "If you were a black man and you could take your family and live anywhere in the entire world...where would that be? England?"

"Jesus...no!" Bond blurted. "Certainly not England. Not anywhere on the European continent I should imagine either."

"How about Africa then? Any country in Africa?"

"Er...no. There are better places..."

"Asia? South America?"

"No. Not really."

"There you have it, then," Uncle Sam said. "The fact is that America is the best country in the entire world for a black man to live and raise a family. There's a reason for that. Certainly, the USA isn't perfect, but the liberty, opportunity and equality we have here is unmatched anywhere else in the world. This is a great country and we want to keep it that way."

The earnest look on Uncle Sam's face floored Gavin Bond. Here was a black man standing up for the liberty and justice of America. To his liberal point of view, this black Uncle Sam contradicted everything he had been led to believe about black America.

Gavin thanked Uncle Sam and moved down Pennsylvania Avenue. His mind roiled with confused thought and conflicting emotion. He had a lot to think about.

What if America was indeed the last great hope for mankind? What if he and all the other progressives were actually on the verge of realizing their lifetime goal of overthrowing capitalist America and replacing it with the European socialist model? All his life he believed that this was the proper thing to strive for. But now he had doubts.

What would happen to the world without America's moral leadership? What would happen to Europe without America's military protection? What would happen to the world economy? Where would the leadership for international cooperation on a host of matters come from?

The United States had led more nations to democracy and liberty than all the others in the world combined. The United States had protected hundreds of millions of people from the oppression of Nazism, communism and dictatorship. The Americans had saved countless millions more from death and suffering from starvation, disease and natural causes. America gave more foreign aid than all other nations in the world combined — even borrowed the money to do it. What would happen if the progressives actually *succeeded* in destroying the America that had brought so much prosperity, freedom and goodness into the world?

His cameraman, Ian, came up to him.

"Boss," he said. "Let's get the set up shots and wrap things up. I'm hungry."

Gavin Bond nodded.

"Righto," he said. "But afterwards I want a drink. I've got a lot of hard thinking to do."

He turned and looked at the hundreds of thousands of people parading in protest up and down Pennsylvania Avenue. "History is being made here, Ian," he said. "And I'm beginning to wonder if we've been on the right or wrong side of it."

17

HOPE AND CHANGE

P resident Barak Hussein Omeba looked out over the podium at the packed auditorium. Valerie Garrotte knew that he would need a carefully managed and fully supportive audience for the most important speech of his career, so she got him the Kennedy Center and filled it with true believers. His trusty teleprompter was there. It held yet another powerfully evocative speech that Dr. Soros had loaded with subliminal messaging. CNN, CBS, MSNBC, ABC and other alphabet soup mainstream media companies were set up to brainstream the speech across America. This was the speech that would define Omeba's Presidency and change the world.

He alone could deliver it. Only Barak Hussein Omeba had the audacity, the charisma, and the oratorical skills to successfully deliver this momentous speech. Only Omeba could mesmerize the crowds so effectively. He was the Anointed One, the Messiah. This was his time to shine in the television lights, and allow the world to receive the blessings of his brilliant oratory. Omeba's smiling face would be beamed around the nation and the world. His glorious shining face would unite the masses, the proletariat, the downtrodden and oppressed. He would convince them to take the great leap forward to win the future for all humankind. Barak looked into the beaming glow of the klieg lights and smiled. This was his time. This was his place. Only *he* could do this. Who was like him?

"Barry...*Barry?*" Valerie Garrotte whispered harshly from behind the stage curtains. "You have to come out of it now. It's time for you to speak. Put your hands on the podium. Look into the teleprompter, Barry. Look-into-the-teleprompter. It will tell you what to say."

The television control booth signaled that they were ready. Valerie nodded for them to proceed. The moment had come. The audience control lights blinked politely to inform the crowd that they must bestill themselves, and give their leader complete attention and respect. They did so. The teleprompter came to life. He cleared his throat away from the microphone and took a sip of water. His head rose. He smiled. There was a twinkle in his eye. Omeba spoke.

"My friends, we live in the greatest nation in the history of the world. I hope you'll join with me as we try to change it."

A thunderous blast of cheering and applause roared from the audience. Barak beamed back at the crowd, basking in their adulation. Then he gave a shy, embarrassed grin as he looked down, in feigned modesty, certain that the cameras caught the moment correctly. He counted the seconds, listening to the roar and detecting the heartbeat of the crowd. The right moment to resume speaking was critical. He was expert at this.

"Change will not come if we wait for some other person or some other time. *We* are the ones we've been waiting for. *We* are the change that we seek."

The crowd roar was deafening. Omeba smiled his famous smile and waved at his people. He had them. He had the crowd in the palm of his hand and he'd just gotten started. This was familiar, comfortable territory to Omeba: ecstatic screaming crowds. He loved it.

"My fellow Americans, I come to you tonight to speak of the three greatest challenges that face our great nation today: jobs, environmental destruction and social justice. Fortunately, we have answers for all three.

"When I ran for the presidency, I ran on a platform of fundamental change for America, and that's what I aim to do. My plan is to remake America as it ought to be, not as it is. The problems we face derive from our economic system and our social values. It's time we faced up to what the real problems are and changed the way we do things. Let's take capitalism for example. Now, it's a simple theory. And we have to admit that it's one that speaks to our rugged individualism and our healthy skepticism of too much government. That's in America's DNA. And that theory fits well on a bumper sticker. But here's the problem: It doesn't *work*. It has *never* worked."

The crowd in the Kennedy Center came to its feet, roaring and screaming at the top of their lungs. This is what they had come for. This was the hope and change that they truly wanted. This was Marxist red meat. This was Socialist soup. The fellow travelers finally heard the words they had craved forever. Their clamor was deafening. President Omeba gave the crowd its few minutes of standing ovation before waving them down.

"Capitalism isn't the answer," Omeba cried. "It's the *problem*. It didn't work when it was tried in the century and a half before the Great Depression. It's not what led to the incredible postwar booms of the '50s and '60s. And it didn't work when we tried it during the last few decades. I mean, understand, it's not as if we haven't *tried* this theory."

The Kennedy Center went crazy with cheers and whistles.

"We can't have social justice as long as we have corporate greed robbing the economic pie from the mouths of the poor. It is true that these big corporations generate most of the money in our economy, but the problem is that they *keep* most of it, too! I have never understood why the business community — whether big business or small business — thinks they can freely take our labor, our roads, our police protection, our government programs, and use them to generate money for themselves. I just don't understand their thinking.

"It's time for us to change our economic system so that the wealth of this great nation is properly managed and equitably distributed — from each according to his ability, to each according to his need. It's time to take the means of production from the hands of the greedy capitalists, and give it to its rightful stewards. And if we *do* these things, we can have free health care for everybody, free housing and free education — all provided by the government at no cost to anyone!"

The Kennedy Center erupted again. Some covered their ears with their hands: the screaming was ear-splittingly loud.

"We can have our worker's paradise by merely increasing taxes a little on the wealthy, and reorganizing our economy with new laws and regulations. The government knows how to take care of people better than greedy corporations...or individuals. Let's try trickle *up* for once instead of trickle *down*.

"Capitalism has never worked because the greedy keep too much of their money. I think that when you spread the wealth around it's good for everybody. We can fix our economy and provide good government jobs for everybody by putting an end to capitalism.

"And do you know what else? We can also fix our environmental problems by ending rampant capitalism. Petroleum and coal are poisoning our world. Big oil and big coal are killing us. The capitalists are making us *pay* them to kill us! Can you *believe* this? We've got to change a few things to straighten this mess out. Energy conservation and new green energy solutions will provide abundant energy and jobs into the twenty-first century."

The audience screamed their approval at these remarks. Valerie had reserved the first six rows for their most rabid environmental donors. This is what they had come for. Their unwavering support for Omeba and the leftist agenda was vindicated at last.

"We are going to live in a world without corporate pollution of our air and water. We will initiate the Cap and Trade program to limit the production of greenhouse gases and killer carbon dioxide. We'll put a tax on every ton of child-killing carbon emitted by the capitalists. Energy prices will, out of necessity, skyrocket. But I have a plan.

"We will build seventy thousand wind farms across this great nation. Think of all the construction jobs this will mean. We'll build a total of seventeen million wind generators, using equipment supplied by our comrades in China. All this for a paltry investment of only seven and a half trillion dollars.

"But everyone will have to make sacrifices if we want to live in harmony with our natural world. We can't drive our SUVs and eat as much as we want, and keep our homes at seventy-two degrees at all times, and then just expect that other countries are going to say okay. That's not leadership. That's not going to happen."

Loud raucous cheers erupted from the audience.

"The Republicans will tell you that this plan won't work. What the Republicans have failed to tell you is that because of global warming, all the weather is going to be more intense: more droughts, more floods, and more hurricanes. That means the wind is going to blow harder. They fail to mention the fact that during my second term, it's going to blow a *lot* harder. Because of this, windmills will generate more electricity than even the Department of Energy knows how to measure. Solar panels will generate more electricity because the wind will blow the clouds out of the way. We will live in a nation where electrical energy will be abundant and practically free. There won't be any more pollution from coal or petroleum. We'll live in a clean green world for the first time. The ocean levels will begin to fall, and the temperature of the world will return to normal. And people will stop dying in the thousands from the poisons the Republicans have put into the water and in the air."

The crowd came to their feet once again, clapping and cheering loudly. Omeba looked sideways at Valerie. Her eyes were shining. Rahm gave him a thumbs-up. Moochelle stood next to Rahm applauding and smiling, giving her husband a sardonic, congratulatory smirk. Even Dr. Soros seemed to approve: He motioned to Omeba to get on with it. Omeba knew that they had reached the heart of the matter. It was time to invoke the action needed to get his program and policies rolling. He raised his hands to bring the crowd back into their seats.

"Now...I'm going to tone it down a little and speak very seriously with you about what we need to do to secure the glorious future that awaits us. You know that there are those who oppose us."

Boos, hoots and hisses.

"You know that there are people who disagree with our politics and our solutions. These Republicans and Tea Partiers, and worse yet...these *Patriots*, have vowed to fight us every step of the way. Now bear with me here, because I'm coming to the heart of our problem. We can't have the higher taxes and more spending we need to get our policies and programs started, *unless* we can stop those who oppose us. We can't have the new laws and regulations we need to get our government to work the way we need it to, because the capitalists will fight us in court, in Congress and on the streets."

Boos and angry murmurs filled the auditorium.

"Bear with me now. The heart of this matter is that we have to win this struggle. Our enemies are capitalist greed and racism. Our enemies are the religious right and social conservatives. If we don't stop them, they'll take our civil rights away from us. We will lose the right to abortion. Homosexuals will be hunted down and killed. We'll lose our rights to welfare, government housing and electronic benefits transfer. They will put our old people out on the streets to die. Our little babies will starve to death!"

The crowd rose to its feet again, shouting *No!* and *Stop them*! A chant rose from the hard-core environmentalists in the front rows: *Fight! Fight! Fight!*

"*That's* the spirit," Omeba encouraged. "That's exactly what we need to do. We need to *fight*. It will be a hard fight. I might not get there to the Promised Land with you, but I'll fight with you anyway. We shall fight them in the streets. We shall fight them in our government offices. We shall fight them at their place of work. We shall fight them in their businesses. We shall fight them in their homes. We *won't* give up. We won't *ever* give up until we win. This is a permanent revolution! We are going to change the United States of America. The time for hope is over. The time for change is now. Now is the time to *fight*."

Fight! Fight! Fight! The crowd shouted back at him.

"Fight!" President Omeba shouted into the television cameras. "You have to fight with me. I won't let you go back to the passive lives you had before. I'm gonna *make* you fight with me. You have to come out of your offices, out of your homes and out of your factories and march with me — through the fire hoses and the police dogs. You have to fight with me. It's gonna be a street fight. It's gonna be nasty! If they bring a knife...we bring a gun. We need a mass uprising to overwhelm the jack-booted thugs who oppose us. Are you *with* me? Are you going to *fight?*"

"Yeah!" the crowd roared. "Hooo! Fight! Fight! Fight!"

And all across the United States of America, millions of people stood in front of their televisions with their fists raised, shouting Fight! Fight! Fight!

The echo was deafening. The walls of the building seemed to vibrate with the loud crashing chant. Fight! Fight! Fight!

Gavin Bond sat at the back of the Kennedy Center in stunned horror at what he had just witnessed. It reminded him of Hitler's famous Reichstag Speech of December 11, 1941. It had the same flavor, the same appeal to the emotions — and ended with the same hate-filled, maniac fervor, and the same call to violence as the speech he had just witnessed. Adolph Hitler declared war against the United States of America in his famous speech. Gavin Bond, the English BBC correspondent, had just witnessed the President of the United States declare war on America.

18

LOST IN ZOMBIELAND

Gavin Bond walked out of the Kennedy Center in a state of shock. The speech President Omeba just delivered to the nation was staggering in its implications. He sat on the steps to collect himself. He couldn't make his mind grasp everything President Omeba had said. He couldn't *believe* what Omeba had said. It made Bond question everything he had ever believed in. The senior BBC commentator considered himself a progressive in good standing: a liberal's liberal — or at least he once did. Now he had serious doubts about the entire prospect of liberalism. What he had been witnessing in the past few weeks in America made him question all of his formerly treasured values and beliefs. Prior to that, his great wish — and the wishes of everyone he knew — was to get a man in the White House who would turn the United States forcibly and irrevocably onto the path of international socialism.

But now that the unthinkable had actually happened, he questioned the wisdom of it all. Socialism didn't fit on America. It was like trying to put an eagle into a monkey suit. America was far better off before the Socialist Internationale and the Democratic Party finally managed to put a fellow traveler in the White House — and pack Congress with them.

The United States had pretty much jumped into every foreign entanglement that it could blunder its way into. But the USA had never invaded another country for the purpose of conquering it, claiming the land and stripping it of its wealth.

Communist nations did this routinely, the world over, and constantly threatened to do more of it. Would a socialist United States forbear the misuse of its vast military power? No. He knew that it would not...could not. There was not a socialist superpower in the world that did not flail at its neighbors and covet their lands.

Gavin realized how wrong he had been about everything. Every smug critical comment he made on BBC programs over the years contributed to the trickle of venom that poisoned the Spirit of America. He felt responsible, in part, for what he was witnessing, and loathed himself for it. These thoughts depressed him utterly.

It was early afternoon in Washington, D.C. Thick cloud cover gave the city a dreary gray overcast. Gavin found his rented car and drove mindlessly through the streets. He had the vague idea of finding a liquor store and his hotel room, and drinking himself into oblivion.

Gavin Bond believed that America was doomed. But in spite of that, or because of it, he felt a strong desire to find his crew and get back to work. He felt an obligation to tell the story, to establish the historical facts before the socialists could write their version of history. So he phoned his news crew with instructions to meet him in front of the White House on Pennsylvania Avenue.

He was astonished to find the streets downtown completely clogged. He abandoned his car and set out on foot for the White

House. Gavin had been in many large crowds before, but never one this large. It was stupendous. He estimated that more than two million people clogged the streets of downtown Washington, D.C. There was barely room to walk. They were a sad bunch of people. Many were crying. Many people were in a daze, and stumbled along mindlessly. They were so lost in their misery that walking among them required care and attention. As he approached Pennsylvania Avenue, the crowd thickened into a crush he had to edge and push his way through.

He saw that people were playing the President's speech over their smart phones and iPads. People gathered together in clumps to listen, angrily denouncing the President's words among themselves. Some were crying and holding onto one another. The people were filled with despair and pain...and anger. It was so sad to see them this way. There was no question of how devastating the President's speech had been to the patriotic masses. Their entire world had been shattered. It was gone.

He walked through LaFayette Park, then across Pennsylvania Avenue in front of the White House. The streets and green spaces were completely jammed with people. He could hear snippets of Omeba's speech as he struggled through the solid knot of bodies. People played the speech over and over, angrily denouncing it, and cursing the President and the Democratic and Republican Parties. They cursed and denounced the Democrats because they had worked ceaselessly for fifty years to bring this socialist hell upon the country, and they excoriated the Republicans for being too cowardly and corrupt to stand up to the Democrats and stop them.

In a thirty-minute speech, President Omeba had refuted the nation's founding values and principles. He declared that capitalism — the historic source of economic prosperity for the nation — was dead. He declared that he would set the nation on a course for socialism, and called for a real class war to see that his goals were achieved. Gavin knew Americans. He knew how they would react to such a speech. There would be fighting. There would be blood.

Gavin could certainly understand why the protesters and patriots hated the speech and were so upset by it. He wondered how the President's supporters would respond to it.

Then he began to notice large numbers of people filtering out of the office buildings that sat back from the street. They came out of the doors and down the granite steps in waves. They came from the Treasury Department and the Eisenhower Executive Office buildings like a great mob of angry robots. Their gait was halting; their expressions blank, and they waded without hesitation into the dense crowds of anti-government protesters. Gavin watched in horror as the groups met. He cursed the fact that Ian, his cameraman, hadn't shown up yet. He took out his iPhone and started recording what he saw.

The mass of government employees walked like zombies into the crowd of Tea Partiers and Patriots. They reached their hands out claw-like for their faces, for their throats, as if to pull the flesh off and choke them to death. This strange attack might have intimidated or driven off a more timid crowd. But the Patriots and Tea Partiers stood their ground and fought back vigorously, many of them cracking their picket poles across the skulls of the government zombies.

It was an astonishing thing to watch: the bureaucrats and office workers in their business suits and ties, attacking blue jean and tee shirt-wearing citizens. There was no question as to who was the aggressor and who the defender. The government zombies attacked the citizen protesters. There was also no question about which side was better at fighting: the government workers went down to the pavement, broken and bleeding. But they were many, and they continued to pour out of the government office buildings.

Even more curious was how quiet the melee was. The zombies said nothing, just snarled and growled. They reached out to grab and throttle. The Patriots grunted with the effort of clobbering government workers. They shouted to one another for help or to warn of an approaching attack. Zombies killed and injured many people, including many women and children. The attacking zombies were dragged off their victims and viciously beaten and stomped.

The Capitol Police were largely ineffective. They couldn't get onto Pennsylvania Avenue in their patrol cars due the crush of people blocking the streets. And when they marched in with their riot gear and batons, they found themselves being swamped by the zombies. Many police owed their lives to the Tea Partiers and Patriots who beat and whacked the zombies off of them.

The Capitol Police called the Marine Barracks and the United States Army at Fort Belvoir for reinforcement. They feared that the rioters might swarm the iron fencing surrounding the White House. But this never happened. The wild fighting in front of the White House, however, became a full-fledged riot. Gavin's iPhone jangled. It was Ian.

"Where are you?" Gavin demanded. "I'm in the middle of a riot in front of the White House. The...the office workers are attacking the protesters! We need video!"

"I'm *getting* video," Ian said. "I'm getting a bloody lorry load of video, Gavin. There's fighting *everywhere* in Washington. Government workers are pouring out of Federal buildings in enormous numbers. You should see them. They're acting like zombies. I'm on Constitution Avenue and heading your way. Have you been on the internet?"

"No. Why?"

"Because the Americans are fighting like this all over the land!" Ian reported. "They're going at it hammer and tongs in New York City, half of New Jersey is up in flames, and there is murder and rioting from Kalamazoo to California. The news everywhere is bloody awful!"

"No, it isn't."

"What?"

"No, it isn't awful news," Gavin cried. "It's the best bloody news there could be! Ha! Don't you see? The Yanks are fighting back! They're fighting back for their country. It's the best possible news in the world!"

19

DON'T TREAD ON ME

Protesters massed outside the White House, surrounding it on all four sides. Huge bonfires from the night before still burned in Lafayette Park. The ten-block area downtown, from the White House to the Capitol, was a charnel house. Bodies lay in neat orderly stacks and lines, dragged to the curb for eventual pickup. People stumbled in and out of office buildings with improvised clubs, looking for zombies.

In other parts of the city the zombies prevailed. They held the areas north and east of the Capitol Building and the surrounding blocks. Fighting continued sporadically in broken pockets of the city.

The Capitol Police and the Marines tried unsuccessfully to move the protesters away from the White House. When the police started arresting people they were attacked, disarmed and driven away. There were simply too many protesters for the police or military to contend with. And there was no rational dealing with the zombies.

The Patriots won the encounter with the zombies, at least the first round. They killed or drove them away. They took their stand in front of the White House, but there were still millions of zombies loose in the city.

The protesters crowded the TV crews to mug the cameras, tell their stories, and get their signs and battered bloody faces on national television. They broke into impromptu chants and speeches about liberty and freedom, and shook their fists at the President and the Democratic and Republican parties. The American people were beyond angry. The situation was completely out of control.

The White House was bunkered down. The Secret Service and the Marine Corps surrounded the executive office buildings with hastily dug machine gun pits. The roofs were lined with snipers and more machine guns. All of them were astonished that the Patriots and Tea Partiers had not rushed the gates and invaded the White House.

The denizens of the White House were filled with fear and foreboding. They stayed glued to monitors for any news concerning the situation outside and around America. The news media coverage of the reaction to President Omeba's speech was shocking. Endless scenes of rioting, mayhem and bloodshed looped constantly on the mainstream networks. The entire nation was at war with itself.

It was compared to the War Between the States. Brother fought brother, father against son, mother against grandmother. The American people fought each other in the cities, towns, villages and byways. Zombies sought out Patriots in roving mobs. Often the mobs would overrun the Patriots en mass, leaving behind broken, trampled bodies. Patriots, for the most part, fought in smaller groups. They formed ambush teams, watch committees and organized themselves for their common defense. Sometimes massed gangs fought one another in bloody, horrific encounters. They fought with clubs and knives, with guns and Molotov cocktails. They fought with cars and furniture and rocks and bottles. From New York to California, the American people fought with their neighbors and family members, with their former coworkers and townspeople.

The Patriots had the advantage of their wits and personal initiative, and they had more guns — thanks to the Second Amendment, the right to keep and bear arms. They took their deer rifles and shotguns from gun cabinets, dusted old war mementos off and oiled them. They found hand-me-down guns tucked away in closets and drawers. The Patriots knew how to handle their weapons and aim them properly. To them, gun control was using both hands.

The Zombie War spread across the continent. There was almost no fighting in Alaska, but Hawaii was a slaughterhouse of blood and gore. Few normal people managed to escape Hawaii. Outside of the large urban areas on the mainland, the zombies were quickly defeated — but they owned all of the major cities. And in the liberal northeast and west coast states, the zombies descended on their defenseless countrymen and wiped them out — men, women and children. But huge bastions of liberty prevailed in the south, west and midwest.

The media coverage was intense in the opening days, then dwindled as the television stations and newspaper offices were torn apart and burned to the ground. The American people knew who their enemies were. By the end of the second week of the Zombie War, the administration had to rely on military and FBI intelligence feeds to determine how the fighting was going.

The nation's Patriots gathered themselves and began a major march on Washington, D.C. to confront the government. The administration well understood that the majority of the people were in revolt against President Omeba's declaration of socialist revolution and warfare. But nobody knew what was going to happen next. The media and liberal establishment looked to President Omeba for leadership, but none was forthcoming.

Omeba did realize the magnitude of his error. His speech had been a tremendous folly. Dr. Soros miscalculated the effect the speech would have on the American people. He thought that the progressive zombies would smother whatever resistance there was. It was a gamble, a risk the Inner Circle agreed to take. But they severely misjudged the character of those they governed. Omeba's presidency began coming apart at the seams only days after delivering his fateful speech.

Valerie Garrotte found Omeba sitting in a chair in the Monica Lewdinski Room with his head against the wall, staring into space. The Air Force officer standing next to him with the nuclear football gave her a worried look.

"He's been like this for the past hour," the officer said. "He won't answer questions or speak to me. I hope you can bring him out of it."

Valerie was not sure she could. His spells had been getting longer and more severe lately. She got him up and gingerly walked him back to the Oval Office. She sat him down behind the Resolute Desk and murmured comforting words to him. He acted like she wasn't even there. He was away...in his mind somewhere. She desperately hoped he wasn't thinking about the French Revolution.

Liberals thought about the French Revolution a lot. The French Revolution gave the progressives their ideals of *Liberté, Egalité, Fraternité*, which were later translated into the socialist notions of statist control, collectivism and social justice. The Revolution inspired progressives to think of themselves as Robespierre doing the work of the Committee of Public Safety. The Terror that their fellow travelers visited on the common citizens, elites and royalty of France was justified as virtuous good works. But, when Robespierre's fellow citizens had enough of his *Liberté, Egalité, Fraternité*, they put him under the guillotine, too. The great fear of all leftist revolutionaries was the certain knowledge that revolutions always ate their children.

Omeba feared the people. He feared them greatly. He knew that they had the power to throw him down. One of his recurring nightmares was of being chased through the streets by screaming mobs of people. They always caught him and mindlessly tore him apart, ignoring his screams that what he had done was for their own good. He screamed in vain. The mob would not listen to his magic voice. They tore him limb from limb. They ate him.

Omeba knew with certainty that the crowd of protesters gathered outside the White House would not listen either. Some of them were already screaming for his blood. He hoped they did not have a guillotine. He detested them all. And he feared them.

His desk phone buzzed. Valerie answered it. The Inner Circle was waiting for him in the Situation Room. He managed to collect himself. It was difficult. Valerie helped him. He rose and walked to the West Wing and found the Situation Room. Already seated were Joe Bidet, Dr. Winfrey Soros, Rahm Adramelech, Eric Holdup, Leon Panera, Hillary Clitman and Janet Napolitburo.

Omeba found his seat without looking at them. He appeared exhausted, defeated. The man was shaken to his core. The others noted his appearance with alarm and resignation. His bouts of depression were well known within the Inner Circle and the press corps. It was one of many secrets they kept hidden from the public.

What they did not know was that his narcissistic personality disorder triggered bizarre erratic behavior when he experienced any kind of disapproval or rejection. While this explained the love/

terror relationship he had with Moochelle Omeba, it did not entirely explain the undiluted hatred he felt for those who opposed him politically. It did not explain his need to severely punish those who defied him. And now it seemed the entire nation had lined up against him. The American people sought his expulsion from office, and there was no telling what his reaction might be. But those who knew him best expected it would be destructive beyond imagining.

"We've got a real disaster on our hands," President Omeba said simply. He let out a deep sigh and looked tiredly at his Inner Circle. "My speech...was not received properly. They misunderstood me. Instead of inspiring the working class to rise up and fight for social justice, it has stirred up a hornet's nest of Tea Baggers and Patriots. Now we've got a national uprising to deal with. Janet, what are your thoughts about our immediate security needs?"

Janet Napolitburo was prepared. As Secretary of Homeland Defense, she had already implemented a full range of measures and she was ready and willing to do even more to suppress the American people.

"Yes, sir," she said. "We have a man-caused disaster unfolding throughout the whole of the United States. I've declared a Federal Emergency. Code Red. We've mobilized the military and they are ready to move on receipt of the proper authorization. But that's the problem, Mr. President. Eric, can you expand on the problem we're having getting the military into gear on this?"

The Attorney General looked at the President, then the others.

"It's a matter of Federal law and constitutional restrictions," Holdup began.

Omeba rolled his eyes and put his head in his hands. The Constitution had thwarted him since the first day he took office. As a former constitutional law adjunct professor, he had a pretty good idea what the constitutional problems were going to be.

"The Posse Comitatus Act prevents us from using Federal military forces to enforce the law," Holdup said. "That's why we can't use the Army to put down these so-called Patriots who are rioting in the streets. The military refuses to move troops from their bases because of this."

"How about if I gave them a direct order to do so," Omeba asked.

"You would have to declare martial law first," Holdup replied.

"Can I do that?"

"Yes. But its political suicide," Holdup said. "Governors can declare martial law to deal with natural disasters or riots. But no President has done so since Pearl Harbor, and that only pertained to Hawaii."

"But there is a new option," Janet Napolitburo chirped. "Tell him, Eric."

"She's right, Mr. President. The Defense Reauthorization Act you just signed allows us to use the military to arrest and detain terrorists. We can hold them indefinitely and without trial."

"I thought that was just for Al-Qaeda," Rahm said.

"It's for Al-Qaeda, the Taliban and for *those who support them.* The Patriots are terrorists, too," Holdup replied. "It's a legal stretch but I think I can make it work. Under the reauthorization act, all the President has to do is declare the whole of the United States 'a battlefield'. Once he's done that, I can argue that the Patriots support the same goal as Al-Qaeda — which is to overthrow the United States government — and are, therefore, 'supporting' them. We can then legally declare the protesters as terrorists, and use our military forces to arrest and detain them."

"Are you sure we can do this?" Omeba asked.

"Certainly," Holdup said. "The Defense Reauthorization Act specifically allows the United States Army, Navy, Air Force,

Marines and Coast Guard to arrest and detain American citizens on American soil. We couldn't have passed it without the Republicans, and it's a done deal. We can do this."

"But where will we put them all?" the President asked. "Guantanamo will fill up fast if you send the Airborne Rangers out to start picking people up off the street. There must be a couple of million of them outside the White House right now."

"Sir, we've got it all worked out," Janet Napolitburo said. She laid out her plan. "First we have the EPA declare the protest areas a threat to human health and the environment. It's true. The porta-potties are filled up and people are relieving themselves on the streets. There are dead bodies out there rotting away. These people have caused groundwater contamination. I've spoken with Lisa Jackoff and she's ready to declare an emergency environmental disaster. The EPA troops are already on the way. We'll use EPA troops and my TSA army to clear downtown Washington of the public health hazard. That'll deal with our immediate security problem. We'll need to round these troublemakers up and contain them, so I've got FEMA on board with their reeducation camps. We can hold nearly twelve million citizens indefinitely in these camps, and we can build more.

"The Joint Chiefs have said that they're not mobilizing against the citizens but they would provide protection for government buildings inside the district. That's not good enough. But if you officially designate the United States as a battlefield zone, then they'll have the legal authority to move on the citizens. Sir, if you give me the authorization, I'll get started on this," Janet Napolitburo said, standing up. "We can start the troops moving into the cities and towns within twenty-four hours."

"You'll have the President's full authorization by the time you get back to your office," Eric said. He waved a sheaf of papers in his hand. "I've already prepared the order." They both looked at President Omeba, who nodded. Napolitburo gathered her papers and left for her office. President Omeba looked fondly after her.

"Janet's a good man," Omeba observed. "I wish I had fifty more like him."

The others nodded in agreement as Napolitburo left the room to mobilize the nation's federal police forces and the military against the civilians.

President Omeba turned to Dr. Winfrey Soros.

"What happened?" he asked. "What happened to my beautiful speech? Why didn't the workers of the world unite?"

The President looked as if he were about to break out into tears. Soros frowned and looked at his hands on the desk. The popular uprising was his fault. He knew that. While the Inner Circle had agreed to his proposal, he knew it had been premature — and he knew where his error was.

"It was love," he said softly, not looking up.

The others at the table leaned forward, wanting to hear everything.

"Did you say love?" Joe Bidet asked. "You did say *love*, didn't you?"

"Yes," Soros said, looking at the Vice President. "It is as we discussed before. The American people have too much love in them. Certainly there are many who do not. Those are empty people, the lost people, who are easy to lead. They are thirty-five percent of the population. But the real Americans have too much love for their country to give up so easily. I thought the zombies would overcome them. I believed the American people had been so thoroughly weakened by decades of prosperity, moral decay, sloth and television programming that they would be easy to take. But no. Their love of America gives them great strength."

Dr. Soros looked at President Omeba.

"The speech did not win us a quick victory," he said carefully. "But all is not lost. You can win the day for our cause if you resort to oppression. You must do this now, before it is too late. Before the Patriots and Tea Baggers have time to solidify their gains. Before the military can decide which side they will fight for."

"Oppression?" Rahm asked Dr. Soros. "Should I call Janet back?"

"You don't mean real oppression, do you Dr. Soros?" asked Vice President Bidet. "*Do you?*"

Every member of the Inner Circle carefully watched and listened. Dr. Soros nodded, but he spoke only to Omeba.

"Oppression is the final solution for every socialist revolution," he declared. "It is a legitimate tool of warfare. Not a single communist nation on earth rose to power without it. Not one of them. Now it is the United State's turn. The great beast must finally feel what it is like to live under oppression. It is for the good of the people that we do this. President Omeba, call out the army. It is time to march. On to victory, Chairman Omeba. The final solution awaits!"

20

THE PRINCE OF PERSIA

The commando team stole through the darkness of the ancient city of Tarsus, birthplace of the Apostle Paul. It was past midnight and everyone was exhausted, but their quarry was not far away and there could be no rest until they found and captured it.

The commando team travelled in two cargo trucks and a Mercedes taxicab. Captain Laker held his ionizing radiation detector out the front passenger window of the taxi and took a reading.

"It's nearby," he whispered. "We're very close."

"Good," Ariel Hadash said. "I am weary of chasing this nuclear weapon. It is a wonder we have not been challenged by the Turkish authorities by now."

"Then we had better hurry up and get it," Colonel Joel Plummer replied.

The Mercedes taxi sped forward, following the invisible trail of ionizing particles through the meandering cobblestone streets and into a rundown warehouse district. The Israeli driver stopped the car at the curb. The two cargo trucks carrying Seal Team Six pulled over behind them. A moment later the recon squad walked silently past the taxi. The rest of the team waited patiently in their vehicles for a report, which came half an hour later. Colonel Plummer and Ariel listened to the recon team report over the VHF radio. They found the truck. It was parked in a heavily guarded warehouse nearby.

Plummer ordered the Israeli and Seal Team Six commandos forward. They numbered twenty-seven. All were heavily armed. The Americans carried H&K MP submachine guns and M-4 rifles; the Israelis, their suppressed long-barreled UZIs. The commandos moved noiselessly through the streets, hugging the walls of the warehouse buildings.

The warehouse was located in a poor district, with ratty streets and dim lighting. It was a brick and block building with a rusty, corrugated steel roof. The large bay doors were closed, rolled together on tracks. A dim light shone through the windows to the front. From all indications, the Iranian commandos had no idea they had been followed to their hideout.

The recon team drifted back and gave Colonel Plummer, Captain Laker and Commander Ariel Hadash a detailed report. The Special Forces officers quickly decided on a course of action. The sniper team would provide cover fire for the approach. The breaching team would throw stun grenades into the warehouse and break open the door. The assault team would enter the warehouse and kill the Iranian soldiers. They would do this brutally, quickly and as quietly as possible. Prisoners were not desirable. They would take the truck and the bomb intact.

Captain Laker waved the breaching team forward. The radioactive truck was inside, along with approximately twenty Iranian National Guard paramilitary commandos, all heavily armed.

The approach offered little cover. There was certain to be a sentry watching the street. The sniper team used a starlight/thermal imaging scope to scan the glass windows and the large bay doors at the front of the warehouse building.

"Two sentries," the sniper whispered. "I can take them both, but it'll raise a ruckus."

Colonel Plummer nodded to the sniper. After a moment, the sniper's rifle spat twice. The sappers immediately charged the warehouse, broke windows and tossed in stun grenades. Gunfire erupted from the windows. The grenades exploded. Seal Team Six assaulted the building.

The breaching team flung the warehouse doors open wide, then dove back away from the shock of return fire from half a dozen AKS-74 assault rifles. Three hand grenades bounced out of the warehouse and rattled down the cobblestones at their feet. The commandos took cover behind whatever they could find.

Return grenades suppressed the Iranian fire. The allied commandos raced into the warehouse, shooting rapidly in close quarters combat. The truck engine started, then roared as the heavy vehicle gained momentum and rammed through the brick wall. The driver forced the truck through the brick and block debris and onto the street outside.

The commandos chased the truck out of the warehouse for two blocks, firing into the back of the cargo box. The truck tires squealed as the vehicle rounded a corner and passed out of sight. They had lost it again. The nuclear bomb was loose.

People from nearby buildings turned on lights and shouted at one another. Captain Laker's team collected their dead and wounded and loaded them into the trucks for the pursuit. Dead Iranian National Guard commandos lay everywhere. Two Iranians survived the assault. One was deaf and stunned, but unhurt. The other was severely wounded in the stomach. Both wanted to live.

Plummer ordered them loaded up. Seal Team Six resumed pursuit. The ionizing radiation detector showed them which way to go. The truck was on the road for the ancient port city of Mersin, twenty kilometers away. They had to stop that truck. It had a seven-minute head start. Ariel Hadash worked his satellite phone. After a few minutes of Hebrew he was rewarded.

"A man will meet us in Mersin to take the wounded and dead," Ariel said. "The truck might be heading to the docks. Mersin is a major commercial port. If the truck is loaded into a ship it can go anywhere in the world. The Mediterranean Sea leads to all ports. Everywhere."

They sped on through the night.

"You are wounded," Ariel said to Colonel Plummer.

Plummer wiped blood from his forehead and left eye. The eye had been damaged, probably from a grenade fragment. It was a serious wound.

"How bad is it, sir?" asked Captain Laker.

"Not good," Plummer said. "Somebody wrap me up with a battle dressing. I've still got one good eye."

"We will leave you with the wounded in Mersin," the Israeli commander said. He said it kindly and matter-of-factly: it was a regrettable necessity of battle.

"Not on your life," Plummer replied. "I'm going to see this mission through. I'm not hurt *that* bad. One way or another we'll have to end our mission in the next few hours. I'm not going to quit now. We're too close."

"Yes, Colonel," Ariel agreed. "We are close, but we may have much to do before we see the bomb. The Persians are very intelligent...very tricky. It is a mistake to underestimate them."

Plummer had to agree. The Iranians had led his team on a diabolically deceptive and treacherous path, with numerous traps and decoys along the trail. The Iranians had planned this operation thoroughly. It only proved how determined they were to get their nuclear devices to their designated targets.

"Let's find that truck," Plummer ordered.

They barreled down the O-51 highway, skirting Mersin. Captain Laker informed Plummer that he had reacquired the truck with the nuclear emissions detector. They could not see it yet, but knew that it was not far ahead. Colonel Plummer took out his satellite phone and punched in a secure code. He was connected to the Pentagon immediately. He hunched over the phone in intense conversation for ten minutes. On more than one occasion, he barked orders and threatened the operators and officers in the chain of command he was climbing, until finally the satphone beeped into the person he wanted to speak with.

General Dimpey, Chairman of the Joint Chiefs of Staff, was serious and reserved at the beginning of the call. He informed Colonel Plummer that he had been officially disavowed by the Pentagon, and could face court-martial when he resurfaced. Then he congratulated Plummer on intercepting the first Persian Bomb, and expressed the urgent hope that the ultra-secret mission to snatch the last nuke might succeed. He promised to move heaven and earth to get Plummer whatever support he needed. But the situation had changed at the Pentagon and only irregular assets were now available. They spoke for five full minutes. Colonel Plummer switched the phone off and waited. He was sweating. Everyone in the Mercedes stole a look at him. The head wound looked terrible.

Ten minutes later the satellite phone beeped again. This time he was speaking with the Captain of the U.S.S. Spruance — the cruise missile ship that had abandoned him a few weeks earlier. The ship was on station in the Mediterranean, off the coast of Cyprus.

General Dimpey had ordered the new patrol route for the missile destroyer in anticipation of combat support requirements for Operation Persian Bomb. He personally put the Spruance on priority standby status to support Colonel Plummer. General Dimpey instructed the naval officer that he was to obey every order he received from Colonel Plummer, or he would be immediately relieved of command.

Colonel Plummer and the Captain of the Spruance had an intense and earnest conversation — from one professional soldier to another. A million or more lives were at stake. Colonel Plummer informed the naval officer of his requirements. The U.S.S. Spruance would immediately steam toward Mersin and stand by to dispatch shore boats to pick up the commando team — and hopefully a nuclear warhead. The decks of the vessel would be cleared for action. The mission was top priority, ultra-secret and voice-only.

Ariel was unsure how much longer Colonel Plummer could function, however. The battle dressing across his head and eye was saturated with blood. It needed to be changed. There was likely a grenade fragment buried deep in his head or eye, which could be dangerous. He needed immediate medical attention. But Plummer had other ideas.

Ariel's cell phone buzzed. It was their contact in Mersin. He had a covered van and was prepared to rendezvous to pick up the dead and wounded. Ariel informed Plummer, who shook his head. There was no time to spare for the dead or wounded.

"Sir," Captain Laker said. "The truck is dead ahead. We're going to be right on it in less than a minute. I'm alerting the men to be ready for immediate action."

Plummer nodded. Everyone checked their weapons. The Israeli driver rounded a line of buildings and suddenly the great blue Mediterranean Sea stretched out before them. They left the highway and drove onto an access road, through an upscale residential development, and then into a commercial area that ran along the shoreline.

"It's there!" Captain Laker shouted. He pointed to a dock dead ahead. A large, ocean-going ferry abutted the dock. "The signal is different...weaker. But I've got a hot spike of beta particles. There's the truck!"

They saw it almost at once, rumbling across a steel ramp and onto the ferry. The Iranians were expecting them. Iranian Revolutionary Guard commandos rushed up to the ferry wheelhouse with AK-74M rifles. They shot several Turkish sailors who offered resistance, then flooded into the wheelhouse and commandeered the vessel. The ferry blew a blast of diesel smoke from its twin stacks and began to pull away from the dock. The Mercedes taxi and two cargo trucks pulled up onto the dock.

The ferry was less than twenty meters from shore. Bright muzzle flashes winked from the ferry. A line of automatic fire stitched across the taxi windshield, killing the driver instantly. Colonel Plummer and Ariel dove from the rear doors onto the pavement. Seal Team Six commandos opened fire on the retreating ferry, killing four Iranian guardsmen.

The ferry surged through the blue green sea. Now it was sixty meters away and rapidly extending its distance from the men on shore. A Seal Team sergeant led an assault squad to a pair of runabouts bobbing in the water. Two Seal sniper teams fired into the retreating ferry, continuing to kill the enemy.

Ariel yelled for Colonel Plummer, who drew his attention away from the retreating ferry and back to the Mercedes taxi. Captain Laker and the driver lay on the pavement by the taxi. They stared lifelessly at the sky. Commander Hadash was shot in the thigh. The bone was broken but the artery had not been cut. A corpsman tied a tourniquet around the thigh and applied a pressure bandage. Then he injected Hadash with a morphine styrette. Just then a cargo van pulled in behind them. A dozen SpecOps soldiers drew down on the vehicle.

"Don't shoot!" Ariel yelled, waving his arms frantically at the American commandos. "This is our man here in Mersin. He has come to take the wounded and dead...and now maybe the rest of us to safety. Come! We have only seconds before the Turkish police arrive. We Jews cannot be caught here."

Down at the dock, the Seals succeeded in firing up one of the runabout motors. They went to work on the other boat. Colonel Plummer called after them to wait for him. He turned back to the Israeli.

"Take my wounded and dead," Plummer said. "Take the wounded Iranians, too. Torture them. Get everything you can out of them. We're going after the ferry. If we can't get the bomb off the vessel then we'll sink it. That should buy us some time. Stay in contact on the VHF radio. I may need to call you for help."

Commander Ariel Hadash nodded.

"I need the rest of your combat team," Plummer said. "I need them to go with me now."

Ariel nodded again. It was no less than he expected. This American was resourceful, brave and cunning. He had a good chance of recovering the bomb. Hadash cursed the wound in his leg. It was very bad.

"Go with God!" Ariel said, giving the soldier the best blessing he could. Then he saluted.

"Go with God!" Colonel Plummer replied.

He wasted no more time on the dock, but turned and ran to the quay, waving the Israelis over to follow him double quick. The Seals and Israelis piled into the two runabouts, and in seconds the boats were plowing hard through the ferry's wake. In a matter of minutes they were alongside the lumbering vessel, exchanging fire with the Revolutionary Guardsmen on deck.

The Iranians fired down on them from the wheelhouse, killing a Seal unexpectedly. The Seal team return fire blew out the wheelhouse clearview screens and killed everyone in the wheelhouse, including two Turkish crew members and the ship's captain.

Plummer had a hard time shooting and directing his men with only one good eye, but he managed it. His boat was first to come alongside the ferry. They were over the gunwales and racing toward the wheelhouse ladder in seconds. The other boat was alongside moments later.

The Revolutionary Guard commandos were dead by the time Colonel Plummer made it to the wheelhouse. Down on the deck, the remaining Iranians looked to be dead as well. All but one — and he bled profusely from a bullet wound to the back. He was quickly trussed with zip ties. A corpsman applied a tight battle dressing to the enemy's wound and gave thumbs up. The wound was not fatal.

The Seal Team assaulted the cargo truck but it was empty. There was no bomb. Colonel Plummer's tactical radio beeped. It was Ariel.

"We have abandoned the dock," he said. "The Turkish Marines are there now and they will be sending ships to intercept you. Do you have the package?"

"Roger, you have left the dock," Plummer replied. "Roger, the Turkish Marines are after us. I expected that. Negative on the package. The package was *not* on the truck. We're searching the ferry now but I don't expect to find anything. Repeat. The package was not on the truck. I think they pulled a switch on us. We have to keep looking for it, Ariel."

"Roger, negative on the package," Ariel replied. He was exhausted from the mission and his wound. The Iranians had proved to be a canny and resourceful enemy. "I will inform my superiors. We will keep searching for the package. But I must tell you, my friend, I don't think we will find it. I think the Persians have outfoxed us this time. Damn them."

Plummer held the radio in his hand for a few moments, pondering the possibility that Ariel was correct. A commando ran up to him and shouted that there was no nuke on the ferry: that both the Geiger counter and the physical search produced no more than residual radiation from the cargo truck. Plummer informed Commander Hadash.

"What will you do?" Ariel asked. "How will you escape? The Turkish Navy will be on your ferry in minutes!"

"We have a plan," Plummer replied. "You get the wounded to safety and take care of our dead."

He looked at the Iranian prisoner on the deck. The man appeared to be in relatively good shape. He was lucky to be alive, considering a Navy Seal had shot him. The man didn't look like a grunt. He might be an officer. He might know where the bomb was. Plummer would find out what he knew. Waterboarding would only be the beginning.

Colonel Plummer and his SpecOps team made their escape in the runabouts. They had just enough fuel for the hard run to the island of Cypress. The Turkish Navy and Marines could chase after the ferry if they wished. The C-4 charges placed below the waterline and in the engine room were rigged to detonate in twenty minutes. Plummer was taking no chances. If they had somehow missed the nuke and it was still on board the ferry, he was going to sink it. He hoped no Turk would be hurt in the explosion. But Colonel Plummer had more urgent matters on his mind. Seal Team Six had a rendezvous with the U.S. Navy missile cruiser, U.S.S. Spruance. Then they had a bomb to find.

21

THE SUPREMES

The United States government responded to the popular rebellion by unleashing the military on its citizenry. This proved to be an enormous mistake for the government. The Commander in Chief declared martial law. He also declared the entire continental United States to be a 'battlefield'. And then he ordered the Joint Chiefs of Staff to direct all U.S. military forces to report to the President for police duty under martial law. He was met with stiff resistance from the Pentagon. President Omeba fired more than fifty generals and admirals before he found a few willing to order troops into the streets.

The new military commanders quickly learned that most of their subordinate officers, especially those in command of individual military installations, understood their Constitutional obligations better than they, and refused to obey repeated orders to put their troops into action. A handful of military officers, however, actually did order their troops into cities in the Northeast.

In New York City, for example, Mayor Bloom ordered the 10th Mountain Division from Fort Drum to attack and capture the conservative refugees who had barricaded themselves in for a last stand in Central Park. The bewildered troops managed to guard the prisoners and secure the streets from spillover rioting from Harlem. Much to Mayor Bloom's consternation, however, the Mountain Division soldiers had no intention of turning their weapons on their fellow citizens.

Where President Omeba did succeed in using military force against the civilian population, the administration found itself facing a foe with more capability than they could have imagined. The most effective marksmen, it turned out, were not Marine snipers, but deer hunters, who existed in the tens of thousands in every state on the continent. The civilian snipers managed to drive off or scatter most military personnel deployed against the public.

At Fort Campbell, Kentucky, the base commander refused orders to rush his tanks and troops to secure Nashville, a rebel city. He kept his forces on the military reservation and refused to surrender his command to anyone. Dozens of base commanders followed his example.

The military, it turned out, had relatively few people in it who were susceptible to progressive propaganda, and they regarded President Omeba's commands for martial law as a clear violation of their Uniformed Services Oath of Office. The military officers had sworn to uphold and defend the Constitution — not the President.

President Omeba was a Commander in Chief who had no Army, Navy, Air Force, Marines or Coast Guard. He grew deathly afraid of a military coup.

But Omeba had many allies. Those who favored the hope and change of socialism made their mark on the nation in a thousand cruel ways. They wreaked havoc on the transportation system. Union members stopped the delivery of fuel, refused to operate trains and buses or fly airplanes. They ceased loading and transporting mail, packages and goods of any kind. Independent truckers were a notable exception. These brave Americans faced union thugs in hundreds of bloody confrontations across the nation.

Food deliveries became a problem almost immediately. Farmers could not deliver their animals and produce to market. There was no way to process the food, or can, freeze or package it and ship it to the customer. The big cities suffered food shortages almost immediately. Everyone recognized that unless something was done quickly, a worse national disaster was about to overtake the nation.

Looting began as soon as it became apparent that police did not have the numbers to prevent it. Some looting was for essentials, like food, that could not otherwise be obtained. But wholesale looting and rioting consumed entire business districts and shopping malls in all major cities. Government checks ceased to flow. This resulted in nationwide panic, riots and arson. Entire neighborhoods were left to burn to the ground because firefighters could not get past rampaging gangs and gunfire.

Governors called out the National Guard, and some called on the President to send Federal troops into their cities — regardless of the prohibition of the Posse Comitatus Act. Many cities — and all of the major urban centers — suffered widespread fires and looting. The great cities became urban hellholes. Most people kept to their homes and businesses, hoping and praying for an end to the violence and incivility — an end to the Zombie War.

A hard-core constituency of faithful Tea Partiers and Patriots marched and stood guard outside the White House, the Capitol Building and the Supreme Court Building. They wanted those in power to know that the American people had finally had enough, and weren't going to go away. They had fought off thousands of Omeba Zombies and an army of heavily armed troops from the EPA and the TSA. The Patriots stood firm on the ground they had defended at such horrific cost. The battle was for life, liberty and the pursuit of happiness. They vowed to remain until the battle was won.

A battalion of Marines had entered Washington, D.C. but did not molest the Patriots. The soldiers went straight to the buildings they were assigned to guard, set up defensive positions, and eyed the protesters warily. Nobody knew what they would do if it came down to a fight.

Government and elected officials cringed inside the government buildings, amazed that the Patriots outside had not invaded the buildings and hung the occupants. They would have done so in their place. But the Tea Party and Patriot leaders held their angry people back from the bloodbath so many of them craved. The rule of law meant more to them than the fleeting satisfaction that personal revenge might bring. Also, the White House was a precious symbol of liberty and freedom to them. The current occupants had defiled the sacred place, but it could be purified and restored. Constitutional government could return to the Land of the Free.

On Capitol Hill, the Congress of the United States of America stared into the face of violent overthrow. This was what it took to cause the lawmakers to overcome their abject terror of news media disfavor and take action. Over one million angry Americans circled the Capitol. They shouted and marched, chanted slogans and brandished pitchforks and blazing torches. They were mad as hell and weren't going to take it any more.

Congress had as much to fear from the rebels as the administration. It was Congress that had authorized the multi-trillion dollar deficit expenditures and caused the implementation of endless multicultural, politically correct social programs that had bankrupted the nation. It was Congress that had authorized the destructive blizzard of rules, regulations, taxes, fees, penalties, fines, codes and orders that punished and drained the citizens. Too many members of Congress were corrupt beyond measure, and they knew that the public had good reason to want to punish them.

The American people hated Congress. Congress was largely responsible for the nation's state of affairs. Congress made it all possible. President Omeba came from Congress. Most congressmen were smart enough to realize that the worm had turned and was glaring angrily back at them.

Once this realization sank in, several of the Republican congressional weasels put their thick skulls together and contrived ways to protect themselves from the fallout and blowback headed their way.

The congressmen realized, however, that with the people howling in the streets for their blood, that a new law or bill would not be enough. Heads needed to roll. Everyone knew what the problem was. But the votes for impeachment were not there, not even among Republicans. Bold action was required of them. So the Republican weasels did the only thing their collective courage permitted: They filed a lawsuit in federal court.

The Supreme Court was not amused. The lawsuit laid more than six hundred claims against the Omeba Administration for violations of the Constitution, the Racketeer Influenced and Corrupt Organizations Act, the Federal Property and Administrative Services Act, the Federal Acquisitions Regulations, and a blizzard of other federal rules and regulations. One judicial wag remarked that the President deserved to be removed from office because of his blatant substitution of Alinsky's Rules for Radicals for the Rule of Law.

The Supreme Court justices knew that they had to act. A probable factor in their decision was the presence of two hundred thousand demonstrators surrounding the Supreme Court building, many of whom carried torches and pitchforks. Something had to be done by *someone* in government. The other two branches of government had not only failed to act effectively in response to the Zombie War and widespread civil disobedience: they had caused the problems.

But it was not easy for the Supreme Court to agree on what to do. President Omeba had put two of the justices on the court, and they would not hear of any judicial action against him. Nor would they recuse themselves. The Wise Latina lectured her fellow justices that they had no business dictating the terms of the Constitution to the President: he had special immunity, by virtue of a penumbra of a shadow of a dicta derived from *merda taurorum animas conturbit*. His other lesbian appointee was equally discomfited by the notion that President Omeba was in any way bound by the Constitution. He had been operating *ex-constitutio* for the past three years without a single complaint from Congress, the Supreme Court, or the people. She saw no reason to start involving the Constitution at this late date.

In response, the one black justice snarkily questioned whether or not Omeba was bound by the limits of the Constitution at all — because he was not eligible to hold the office of President in the first place.

As the Supreme Court justices argued the matter, this question kept reappearing at the top of the list of potential legal remedies.

The eligibility question became increasingly attractive when compared to the workload involved in dealing with the six hundred individual complaints against the President filed by the House of Representatives. It became even more attractive when balanced against the enthusiasm and determination of the shrieking mob outside.

The question of Omeba's eligibility to hold office bumped and rubbed up against the President's declaration of martial law, the use of Federal military forces to put down the popular rebellion, his usurpation of the Constitutional separation of powers, his circumvention of Congress, his misuse of the regulatory agencies and his unconstitutional use of executive authority.

The act of declaring the entire United States a battlefield, combined with the misuse of technical provisions of the Defense Reauthorization Act, was singularly troublesome. It was despotic. Thousands of innocent soldiers and civilians lay dead as a result of this inconceivable abuse of executive power.

There was no question that something had to be done. Federal buildings were being burnt to the ground nationwide. Cities were aflame and overrun by rioters and looters. The military itself was in rebellion, with most commanders refusing to allow their troops to leave their military bases, and a small number unleashing their men and equipment on the civilian population to horrific effect. The nation was tearing itself apart.

But the Supreme Court was hopelessly divided on the issues that the House presented. The progressive justices would not permit a single vote on the issue of martial law, or the laundry list of Constitutional violations prepared by the House Republicans. There was a potential remedy if the Commander in Chief could be shown to have abused his responsibilities as the nation's top military commander. If Omeba could be relieved of military command, then the rest would take care of itself. But the progressive justices on the court would not allow any argument on this approach either.

This left the Supreme Court with a single viable remedy. The Chief Justice forced a vote on the one question that could resolve all of the other issues: was President Barak Hussein Omeba eligible for the office of President, in accordance with Article II, Section I of the Constitution, which reads as follows:

> "No person except a natural born Citizen, or a Citizen of the United States, at the time of the Adoption of this Constitution, shall be eligible to the Office of President; neither shall any Person be eligible to that Office who shall not have attained to the Age of thirty-five Years, and been fourteen Years a Resident within the United States."

The issue of where the President was born was buried under three million dollars worth of legal interference, blurred history, altered records and mainstream media denial and obfuscation. The President of the United States had never produced an original long form birth certificate, and in all likelihood, there was not one that *could* be produced. It could take a year to sort the birth certificate mess out and arrive at a vote.

But the President himself had declared that his father was Barak Omeba, a Kenyan. The question then became whether or not being a natural born citizen required that both parents be American citizens at the time of Omeba's birth. This was an easier question to answer and there was ample, clear legal precedent to enable the Supreme Court justices to render their verdicts on the question. The Wise Latina and the Other Lesbian shrilly argued that the definition of natural born citizen was something altogether different from what legal history, case law, the writings of the

Founders, the wording of the Constitution and common sense said it was. Argument on the question lasted two days.

By a vote of five to four, the Supreme Court declared that President Barak Hussein Omeba was not a natural born citizen, according to the definition of the term in Vattel's *The Law of Nations*, and Supreme Court precedent in *Minor v. Happersett*, et al.; and was, therefore, ineligible to be President of the United States.

The Supreme Court ordered that all executive orders, laws, rules, policies, regulations, appointments, decrees, and all of his official actions be declared null and void.

The Supreme Court ordered the immediate suspension of martial law, and ruled as unconstitutional the recent Defense Reauthorization Act, in its entirety. The court ordered the Congress of the United States of America to implement the Constitutional rules of succession for the Executive Branch.

Joe Bidet became President of the United States of America.

22

ATOMIC JIHAD

The missile destroyer U.S.S. Spruance was subordinated to Special Operations Command the moment Colonel Plummer boarded the ship. The warship fished Colonel Plummer, his commando team, and an Iranian prisoner out of the Mediterranean Sea, thirty-three days after Plummer's commando raid on the Iranian supertankers in the Suez Canal. The U.S.S. Spruance found Seal Team Six adrift in the runabouts halfway between Mersin and the eastern tip of northern Cypress. The commandos were exhausted and bleeding, and the runabouts had run out of fuel.

Plummer greeted Captain Ellis formally and was granted permission to come aboard. But in fact, the U.S.S. Spruance and her crew were now subject to the SpecOps commander's orders.

Captain George Ellis, commander of the U.S.S. Spruance, had trained at the Annapolis Naval Academy and been thoroughly indoctrinated into the Navy's spit polish and politically correct culture. He did not like having a rogue Seal Team on his missile destroyer. But the choice given him by General Dimpey was to obey every order Colonel Plummer gave him, or be immediately relieved of command. Ellis followed his new orders, but he didn't like them and he didn't approve of the scruffy and dangerous looking Special Forces soldiers roaming free on his ship. All of the SpecOps warriors sported ragged uniforms, unshaven faces, and the dirt, grime and blood of combat. They were heavily armed and extremely dangerous.

Colonel Joel Plummer was particularly wild looking. In the past weeks he had forced his mind and body to the limits of human endurance, and it showed. He looked ragged. His left eye was bandaged and patched over, giving him a sinister piratical appearance. Nevertheless, the man projected command authority. He required combat discipline from the ship's company and officers. When he gave orders to them he expected immediate and complete obedience. He put the ship on full military alert, including manning the deck guns. He ordered Captain Ellis to inform the Turkish Navy that the ship was on combat status and would not respond to any further queries.

Plummer dispatched with the tactical disposition of the battleship as quickly as he could. He saw to it that the remnants of Seal Team Six and the Israeli commandos received medical attention and accommodations. His primary interest was the wounded Iranian prisoner he had brought on board. The ship's doctor treated the Muslim's bullet wound to the back, which had scored deeply through the muscle. The wound was grievously painful. The prisoner was given the best of care, including a halal meal, a Koran and prayer time, but no painkillers. Plummer wanted the Iranian amenable to interrogation. Captain Ellis believed that the way the Colonel treated the Iranian prisoner would likely get them both brought up on charges, but said nothing.

***

The Revolutionary Guard officer was a true believer who had done his best to light the nuclear fire for the return of the Mahdi. The man wanted martyrdom and his seventy-two virgins. He got Plummer, a mouthful of broken teeth, and an intramuscular shot of clear liquid that made him more tractable.

Even then, he did not give up information readily. Plummer resorted to sterner measures. He used his SOG knife, a long flat board, a plate of raw bacon and a gallon of water. The Iranian at first seemed perplexed by Plummer's arrangements, but soon gained the most intimate understanding of their purpose.

By the time Plummer had worked his way to the bone, the Iranian was begging to reveal to the officer any information he desired. With the help of the Israeli commandos, Plummer learned from the Iranian that the truck they had followed into Turkey was a decoy. The Iranians placed half a ton of uranium centrifuge tailings into a stainless steel drum. The drum was perforated to allow radioactive particles to escape, leaving an invisible trail of radioactivity in its wake.

The real nuclear device was taken to the port of Mersin as well, but in a different truck and by a different route. The real bomb was in a hermetically sealed, leakproof container on a cargo truck identical to the one they had been following. While Seal Team Six chased the decoy truck to the ferry, the real bomb was being unloaded at the Port of Mersin. At a modern commercial warehouse there, the nuclear device was prepared for its final journey. It was tested to ensure that it would not activate any airport nuclear detectors. The bomb was fitted with a special altitude detonator, and a broadband radio signal jammer was incorporated into the equipment package. The nuclear device was placed on a hydrofoil and sped to Athens, where it was loaded into the cargo hold of a Lufthansa passenger airliner. Its destination was Houston, Texas.

Once Plummer and the commandos had the truth out of the Iranian, the prisoner collapsed into hysterical laughter.

"You fools!" he screamed at the astonished American soldiers. "It's too late. You can't stop it now. How much will oil be worth to you afterwards? Yes? How much will you pay for gasoline when you can no longer produce it yourselves? Ha! We have brought America to its knees. You have no oil now. And the Mahdi is coming for you!"

Plummer raced to the Bridge to send a top-secret urgent message to Washington. He gained immediate access to the Pentagon.

"General Dimpey the news is very bad," Colonel Plummer said.

"You found the last bomb?"

"Negative, sir. The Iranians slipped it past us. The Prince of Persia bomb is on the way to Houston on board a passenger jet."

"Oh my God! Are you sure? Houston? Not New York City? Not Washington?"

"I hate to say this, General Dimpey, but I'm certain the bomb is on a Lufthansa passenger airliner bound from Athens to Houston," Plummer said. "General, you may have to scramble a jet and shoot it down."

"Shoot down a civilian air liner?" General Dimpey cried. "Are you serious?"

"General, please listen to me," Colonel Plummer pleaded. "Get the Air Force and Navy working a solution to the problem. Find the Lufthansa jet and try to contact it. We may not be able to. The nuke package has a radio jammer. See if you can divert it somewhere...maybe into the Caribbean or the Gulf. Get them to put the aircraft down in the sea. Once you've got the aircraft located and the military options in place, call me back."

There was a long pause on the other line.

"General, there isn't much time."

"I know," General Dimpey said. "Good work, Colonel. For your information, I'm no longer Chairman of the Joint Chiefs of Staff. If fact, *technically* I'm no longer in the Army. I've been canned. But don't worry. My passcodes are still working. Some of us are pushing back. I'm still in charge of some things. And I can find the Lufthansa and bring it down if we have to. I'll get back to you after I've got people working the problem."

"Thank you, sir. Plummer out."

Colonel Plummer was stunned by the news General Dimpey had just shared with him. There must have been some high level shakeups at the Pentagon. He'd been out of the loop for weeks. He hadn't seen a news report in that entire time.

Captain Ellis sat down next to Plummer and held out a cup of strong coffee. He realized he needed to catch the SpecOps commander up on the latest news. There had been many sudden changes in the world since Plummer was assigned to spearhead Operation Persian Bomb. After three cups of ship's coffee, Plummer could put more pieces of the puzzle together. Now he knew why Captain Ellis' missile cruiser abandoned his commando mission while they were engaged in action with the Iranian supertankers. He now understood why the military jerked support out from under the Israelis in the middle of their combat assault on the terrorist camp in the Bekkah Valley.

It was the White House. The President had countermanded Operation Persian Bomb. President Omeba had given the countermanding orders to combat units while they were actively engaged with the enemy. He'd suspected as much, but couldn't make himself believe that a President would actually *do* such a thing. He should have known better. This interference had the very real effect of helping the Iranians sneak a nuclear weapon into the United States. Whether it was by incompetence or design would not matter to the millions of innocent people who would be killed by the nuclear blast.

Hours passed but neither officer left the bridge. They drank coffee and talked. Plummer sent the ship's doctor to check on his men. Time dragged on. When the secure comsat phone beeped, Ellis and Plummer jumped. Plummer snatched the handset from the operator.

"Colonel Plummer here."

"General Dimpey. I've got two F-15s on an intercept mission as we speak. They'll be able to deliver missiles on target in minutes. But we can't get White House authorization to shoot down the airliner."

"What? Plummer gasped. "Are they refusing to issue the order?"

"Well...nobody's answering the phone," Dimpey said. "We've sent Code Red messages via the Secure Hot Line and have receipt of them. Messages are getting to the President's people. I sent two officers directly to the White House to brief the President but they can't get to him. We think he's holed up in there. My problem is that the Air Force commandant refuses to kill the jet. I told him that it was carrying a nuke set to go off over Houston, but he says he needs a confirmed order from the President for missile launch. I can't blame him. That is our protocol. But we have a special situation, and I thought I'd be able to talk him into going forward. He won't do it. The chain of command is a mess. Nobody knows what to do."

Colonel Plummer slumped in his chair. The accumulated tension from the last few weeks drained from him in that long moment. He was exhausted, spent. He rubbed his forehead tiredly. Dried blood flaked to his hand.

"Did you tell the Air Force general what a twenty kiloton nuclear bomb would do to Houston?"

"I did."

"Did you tell him that the EMP from the blast would fry all of the electronics in Texas and surrounding states? Did you tell him that all of our oil drilling platforms in the Gulf and all of the refineries and chemical plants would be knocked out of service?"

"I told him. He insists on getting an order from the President."

"Is there anyone else you can send? Does the Army have any aircraft you could order up?"

"We're working on that now," Dimpey said. "But we're just about out of time. The Lufthansa jet is less than ten minutes out of Houston."

"Divert the jet."

"We tried. No dice. We can't communicate with the jet. The Iranians thought this mission through very carefully. They put a wide spectrum radio jammer on the jet with the bomb. That clinches where the bomb is, as far as I'm concerned. We're screwed."

"Put the F-15s on the airliner's wings," Plummer said. "Force the Lufthansa to divert. Put them in the Gulf of Mexico."

"We're trying that now," Dimpey replied. "But I don't think it's going to work. The F-15s went to afterburners just to get into missile range. We burnt our remaining fuel up waiting for a fire order from the White House. The fast movers will be burning fumes in minutes. The pilots are going to try it, though. Maybe they have enough fuel and time to get the message across to the Lufthansa pilots. It's a long shot at this point."

"You've got to get through to the White House," Plummer said. "You've got to get through. Doesn't the Navy have anything in range?"

General Dimpey sighed. Plummer had a bad feeling about how this was going to turn out.

"I've been trying, Joel," Dimpey said. "I've been trying for three hours to get through to President Omeba. It's no use. Nobody can get through to him. He's not even interested in listening. And negative on the Navy. I tried. The Naval Air Stations are too far away. Same for the carriers. Everything they've got has been sent to the Persian Gulf. The Iranians are trying to close the Strait of Hormuz. There's a hell of a sea battle going on there."

"It's a diversion!"

"You bet it is. And it worked."

Plummer had no response to that. He'd learned to respect Iranian military sagacity in recent weeks. And he'd had his own dealings with the President. Both were intractable. Checkmate.

"One moment," Dimpey said. "I'm getting an update." General Dimpey went off the line.

Colonel Plummer looked gravely at Captain Ellis. The situation could not be more serious. General Dimpey was back on with him in minutes.

"No go, Joel. Our F-15 pilots had to eject. They got to the Lufthansa but it veered away from them. The fast movers ran completely out of fuel trying to catch them."

There was a long silence.

"What's going to happen next, General?"

General Dimpey sighed. "The United States will lose one of its major ports and forty percent of our petroleum supply. It was a mistake concentrating so many oil refineries in Louisiana and Texas. But the environmentalists drove them out of the other states. Now we'll pay for it. It's what will happen to the rest of the country that I'm worried about now. You come home, Colonel Plummer. America is about to go through some serious hell. We need you here."

"I'll report to you as soon as I can get home," Plummer said. "Goodbye, General Dimpey."

Plummer hung up the handset. He and Captain Ellis waited together in the Spruance's command center. A tactical map of the Gulf of Mexico was projected on the main screen. The image was zoomed in over Texas. Military satellites tracked the Lufthansa flight across the map. The Navy Captain and Army Colonel sipped their coffee and waited. They looked at one another. They did not have to wait long.

The white light that appeared over the Lone Star state was brighter than any star that had ever been seen.

23

RED, WHITE AND BLUE

The world was boiling with trouble, rumors of war and open warfare. There was rampant warfare in the Middle East. Egypt, Libya, Tunisia, Syria and Lebanon collapsed into religious civil wars. Christians, Jews and Hindus suffered massive slaughter in these nations. Shia fought Sunni in bloodthirsty battles in Iran and Iraq. The Mahdi had risen from his well.

The United States Navy fought a hideous war with the Iranians to reopen the Strait of Hormuz. The Suez Canal remained closed for weeks after a mysterious tanker explosion shut the waterway down. Speculators kicked up the price of crude oil from $82 to over $700 per barrel. The economic shocks reverberated immediately throughout the world economy.

Food distribution and agriculture came to a halt. There was no diesel fuel to run the engines of commerce and agriculture or to transport their products. Labor and food riots exploded across the third world. Mass starvation threatened the continents of Africa and Asia. People in developed nations desperately hoarded food.

China's blue water navy ventured forth from the China Sea. Japan went on a war footing when the Chinese landed on the Kuril Islands, claimed by both Russia and Japan. Chinese war vessels patrolled provocatively outside the Panama Canal and ventured unchallenged into the Mediterranean Sea.

Russia surprised and horrified Europe by rapidly moving major elements of the Ground Forces of the Russian Federation — including five divisions of T-90 main battle tanks — through Belarus and up to its border with Poland. General of the Army Nikolai Makarov then announced that Belarus and the Ukraine were summarily inducted into membership in the Russian Federation. The old USSR was growing again, the old fashioned way — by annexing neighboring nations.

The People's Republic of Venezuela launched a bizarre incursion across the border into Colombia. Argentina invaded the Falkland Islands. Again. Pakistan threatened nuclear warfare with India. European jihadis rose in England, France, Germany, Italy, Belgium, The Netherlands, Sweden and Denmark. Spain was overrun and in flames. Many jihadis believed that the thirteenth Imam had risen from his well and the War of the Last Caliphate had descended on the world. They joined their brother jihadis in the hundreds of millions to fight and kill the infidel across the whole of Europe, Asia, Africa and South America.

The entire world had gone insane. America had her own problems.

President Omeba declared an extraordinary national emergency. This was in addition to the martial law he had already declared. He suspended the deliberations of Congress. This was possible only with the support of Democrats in the House and Senate, who agreed to boycott the official sessions and deny the Republicans a quorum.

By executive decree, he suspended the proceedings of the Supreme Court and sequestered the justices from public view. The justices never had a chance to announce their historic decision on Omeba's ineligibility to serve as President. Rahm suppressed all knowledge of the monumental court session. He met with the Supreme Court justices and told them that they had a nice Supreme Court there — and that it would be a shame if anything was to happen to it. Rahm coldly informed them that if any one of the justices ratted the President out, they were all going to end up at the bottom of the Potomac River wearing cement overshoes. They believed him.

Problems still existed in the military, which Omeba had yet to bring under his control. But he kept them busy digging out the survivors in Texas and waging war in the Persian Gulf.

The nuclear blast over Houston killed one and a half million people immediately. Another one or two million were expected to die from fires, exposure, radiation sickness, and other causes. The electromagnetic pulse from the Persian Bomb reverberated back from the magnetosphere and plunged most of Texas and Louisiana into darkness. The border regions of Oklahoma and Arkansas also suffered massive damage.

The electromagnetic pulse fried solid-state electronics in cars and trucks, aircraft, ships and trains. All equipment with solid state controls and motors failed, including all elevators, air conditioners, refrigerators and all industrial electrical control systems. Virtually all computers and telephones, televisions and radios were destroyed. All of the chemical plants and oil refineries were shut down, as there were no process control systems, pumps, mixers, compressors, distillation columns, catalytic crackers or other equipment left operational.

Forty percent of the nation's jet fuel, kerosene, and diesel fuel was shut off, as well as fifty percent of the higher distillates, including gasoline. Chemical plants that made fertilizers, pharmaceuticals, plastics and personal care products experienced catastrophic shutdowns. All the water treatment and sewage treatment plants failed. All power plants were knocked offline. Most household appliances were fried. Almost all of the hospitals in the affected region ceased to operate. It was a disaster of the first order.

The rest of America responded immediately. First responders, National Guardsmen, the Red Cross, and volunteers from across the nation flooded into Texas and Louisiana, eager to help their fellow countrymen.

The millions of protesters in Washington, D.C. filtered out of the nation's capital. The nation was under attack. They had to go defend her. They had to go home, or to Texas. Americans stopped fighting one another. The news media admonished the rebels to rally behind the government and support the President in this time of great national crisis.

The media and government urged them to go home and rebuild America; to go home and contribute to the war effort; for a deadly enemy had attacked the homeland and every patriotic American was needed for the nation's defense. The Patriot rebels reluctantly heeded the call. The Zombie War fizzled out. There was a dangerous foreign enemy to fight now. The mainstream media warned that other nuclear blasts could be expected anywhere in the country. Nobody wanted to be far from home when that happened.

President Omeba sat behind the Resolute Desk in the Oval Office and pondered the briefing he had just been given by his Inner Circle.

The scenario they presented the President was astonishing: Omeba could ride out the national emergency and remain in power. They could even postpone the next election cycle. Rebuilding the mainstream news media became their top priority. They would need it if they were to accomplish anything. President Omeba would need to promise the American people many things in order to buy the time he needed to reconsolidate his power base. Fortunately for President Omeba, the Persian War was upon the nation and her Commander in Chief was desperately needed.

To maintain power, all he had to do was ensure the silence of the Supreme Court and make a few more deals with the new military leadership. The military was the more serious problem. Too many military officers knew too much. They could not be bribed, at least not effectively, and threatening a military officer carried it's own peculiar risks. His advisors suggested a purge of non-loyal officers. Some would have to be hunted down and silenced permanently. But all of this was within the realm of possibility. It had been done before. Stalin did it. So did Lenin, who was also a lawyer. So did Mao, Pol Pot, Castro, Amin, Guevara, Ho Chi Minh and many others. Eliminating the opposition was something both Rahm and Omeba understood well: it was the Chicago way.

The Iranians had dropped an administration-saving, nuclear bonanza in their lap. It was the crisis Rahm had wanted so badly. It was their salvation. The nuclear attack on the United States effectively diverted America's attention from the horror and hell of the Zombie War. The news media would help the administration bury that nasty episode. Nobody mentioned the two weeks of insanity that followed the President's seminal speech on creating a socialist America. Everyone in the nation was focused on helping to save as many Texans as they could. And they were focused on fighting the treacherous enemy who dared place a nuclear weapon on a civilian airliner.

Despite administration efforts to deflect blame from the Muslim world, everyone knew that putting bombs on civilian aircraft was a favorite tactic of the Islamists. Americans were sick and tired of Muslims killing innocent civilians and waging constant jihad against non-Muslim nations.

The United States of America faced its most serious crisis. President Omeba decided to ride the people's anger instead of taking the brunt of it himself. It was an administration-saving opportunity for Omeba and he took it.

In a special television address to the nation, President Omeba announced to a stunned America that it was the revolutionary government of Iran that had placed the bomb on the Lufthansa passenger plane that detonated over Houston. The television presentation was meticulously arranged. He called a joint session of Congress and spoke from the House Chamber. Omeba gave a fiery speech, admonishing all Americans to put aside their differences and join together to fight the common enemy. The United States of America went to war.

And this is what saved the Omeba administration. Omeba would wag the dog. He would use the pretext of war with the Iranians as a diversion to cover up what he had done. He would refocus the American people on the external enemy. It was the oldest trick in the dictator's handbook. And it would work.

Valerie asked the President if he shouldn't let some of the Democrats in Congress know what he was up to. He still had strong support among the large number of Democratic socialists in Congress, and they would do anything to help him weather the political tsunami that had engulfed his administration.

"One thing I've learned in my political career," Omeba replied, "Is that if you want to anger a conservative, you tell him a lie; if you want to anger a liberal, you tell him the truth. I'm not about to tell my colleagues the truth about *any* of this."

Rahm agreed.

"I'm convinced you're right, Mr. President," he said. "The fewer people who know what's actually going on, the better. It's easier to control them that way."

"Yes," Omeba agreed. "But we've got to go several steps further. We almost lost power because a small faction of right wing patriots began to dissent. We have to put an end to that. No more backtalk from the chattering classes. No more dissent."

"But what about the First Amendment?" asked Eric Holdup. "The Constitution will prevent us from interfering with legitimate protest."

President Omeba turned to his Attorney General. His face was stern, resolute.

"That's the point I'm making here," he said. "We can't abide the First Amendment. We'll just have more trouble if we tolerate it any longer. In fact, the entire Bill of Rights is in the way, not to mention the rest of the Constitution. We just don't need those archaic documents any more. They stand as a barrier to everything we're trying to accomplish."

"But the people won't stand for it," Holder objected. "The Supreme Court will fight us."

Omeba seemed amused by this.

"The Supreme Court?" he asked. "You mean that band of quivering black-robed cowards I have locked up in their marble building? Nine people? We can disappear them and they know it. We have nothing to fear from the Supreme Court. Rahm took care of them the Chicago way."

"And Congress?" Janet Napolitburo asked. "If they cut off funding for what we want to do, then we're dead in the water."

"We have to worry about Congress least of all," Omeba replied easily. "The institution is so thoroughly corrupt they'll do anything we want. The RINOs will help us. I've already gotten strong messages of support from them. They're eager to go to war and rev up the military industrial complex. They'll do well out of this war. They'll be lapping at the trough like the rest of them in a matter of weeks. Congress won't be a problem."

Rahm looked around the Oval Office. It appeared that the President had thought things through very carefully. Who knew what would really happen? Rahm didn't think they had an ice cube's chance in the hell that had surrounded them the past few weeks. And now they were back on top.

"So that's our plan," Rahm summarized to the Inner Circle in the Oval Office. "We're going to lie our way out of this mess and right back to the height of power. That's what we do best. With any luck we should win reelection...*if* we decide to *hold* any more elections."

He looked at his friend Barry. They both knew that it would be in the second term that they would finally put an end to the beast once and for all.

"Yes," President Barak Hussein Omeba said. "We will continue to lie to them. When the government lies to its people, and there is nothing they can do about it, then that changes them. The people begin to understand how little power they really have.

"I think when you lie to people's faces and force them to be silent about it, that this breaks their spirit. And when you can finally make them repeat those lies, and put the lies into effect in their work and everyday lives, then this affects their ability to perceive reality. Or to even care what reality is. Being lied to constantly erodes the human spirit until there is nothing left but a soft malleable putty that we can mold and shape into anything we want."

He paused for a moment. "We will need a Propaganda Czar to organize the media programming."

"How about a *Minister* of Propaganda?" Valerie offered. "Might as well make it a cabinet-level position."

"That could work," Rahm said thoughtfully. "I'm thinking also that we'll need a Minister of Collectivism as well. In fact, we've got a whole new government to build."

"What about the Constitution?" Eric Holdup asked. "Americans need a Constitution."

"I agree," President Omeba said. "We'll write a new Constitution for America, only this time we'll ensure that social justice is part of the document. The right *kind* of social justice, of course," he said, winking at them.

They laughed. It was good heart-felt laughter, a welcome and much needed cathartic after the weeks of high stress and drama they had all been through. They looked at one another. The triumph of victory shined in their eyes. What they had worked so long and hard for was finally coming to pass. The path forward was open to them now. It would be a difficult road, but there were many fellow travelers to help with the labor. It was time for the proletariat to rise up and throw down the capitalists. The time for hope and change had come at last.

A MESSAGE FROM J.T. HATTER...

Thank you for reading Lost in Zombieland. I hope you enjoyed it. But more importantly, I hope you took something away from the book that you will do something with.

I had to think long and hard about writing this book. I knew it would be controversial. I knew there were certain dangers attendant to writing a book that lampooned and ridiculed the liberal establishment. But in the end I knew I had to do it.

I talked it over with my wife and she agreed. I thought about my children and their future as Americans. I had to do something. The United States of America is in serious trouble. It is time for every one of America's true sons and daughters to come to her defense.

So I wrote *Lost in Zombieland* as a first step.

If you invested the time to read this book, it is likely that you are not to be numbered among the passive. It is likely that you love freedom and liberty and are willing to defend and recover what is rapidly slipping away.

Ronald Reagan once said, "Above all, we must realize that no arsenal, or no weapon in the arsenals of the world, is so formidable as the will and moral courage of free men and women. It is a weapon our adversaries in today's world do not have."

This statement has been proven true from the moment of 'the shot heard 'round the world' to the present. I ask you to join with me, and countless other Americans, and take a stand for freedom and liberty. America needs you.

JT Hatter

John Thompson Hatter
www.lostinzombieland.com
Facebook: JT Hatter
Twitter: @JT Hatter